Christmas
And Other
Inconveniences

TRACY BROEMMER

USA TODAY BESTSELLING AUTHOR

CHRISTMAS AND OTHER INCONVENIENCES

A GRUMPY SUNSHINE, OPPOSITES ATTRACT, FRIENDS TO LOVERS, SMALL TOWN ROMANCE

BETTING ON CHRISTMAS

TRACY BROEMMER

Christmas and Other Inconveniences

by

Tracy Broemmer

Contemporary Romance

Published by Tracy Broemmer

Edited by Lexie Broemmer

Cover by Beck & Dot

For my bridesmaids-
Jackie, Michele, Kim, Beverly, & Laura

And for the brides I stood with at the altar-
Jackie, Michele, Kim, Beverly, & Amy

The things you do for your besties! Love you all!

ABOUT CHRISTMAS AND OTHER INCONVENIENCES

Jessica Bradshaw needs a date for her friend's big city wedding. With her safe dates all busy on that fateful weekend, she's running out of time.

Everyone in Holly Creek, New York, knows about the crazy bet Chelsea Calhoun's bridesmaids and Rex Buchanan's groomsmen made, including Hayes Kelley, Jessica's boss. Hayes is happy to offer up single men in Holly Creek for her consideration, but he has no interest in being her wedding date—mainly because he has no interest in weddings.

Still, as her boss and friend, Hayes knows showing up at the wedding without a date will goose Jessica's anxiety through the steeple of that big city church. How can he not give in and offer to be her date just to get her through what could be a horribly nerve-wracking weekend for her?

Jessica's doubtful at first. Hayes Kelley at a wedding? And yet, the idea grows on her. He might be grumpy and set in his ways, but after working with him for the past ten years, she knows him well, and his presence at the wedding would be a comfort to her. They might even have fun together.

But what happens when the two of them willingly cross the line of friendship and find themselves in foreign territory? Will the wedding of the century end ten years of friendship for Jessica and Hayes? Or will they admit there just might be more to their relationship?

Introducing: The Betting On Christmas Collection

A big city billionaire with a bride from a small town.

A high society New York City wedding with a momzilla being bossy boots.

And a bridal party with one crazy bet.

Will the bridesmaids and groomsmen find their own dates to the wedding of the century this Christmas, or will they all fall victim to Momzilla's decree?

Find out in the Betting on Christmas romance collection by ten bestselling authors.

READ THE PREQUEL

"You are cordially invited to the bridal party mixer in honor of the wedding of Chelsea Calhoun & Rex Buchanan."

Oh dear, what's a bride to do when the bridal party just won't mix?

It's like country versus city and Chelsea is losing hope. The bridesmaids, her small town besties, aren't that amused by Rex's old buddies from New York City. No amount of effort helps, even though Rex offers to force his guys to toe the line.

Enter Miriam Buchanan-Astor, Rex's mother, who's been a momzilla from day one, and this bridal party mixer is a catastrophe. While she's trying to micromanage matchmaking between bridesmaids and groomsmen, they aren't having it.

With everyone at odds, only one thing might save the day *and* the wedding: **A Christmas bet.**

You don't have to read the prequel to the collection, but it's a fun short piece that introduces the Christmas bet.

Read it free here.

CHAPTER 1

*J*essica

"What about Kelley Green's?" Jessica asked as she jotted a reminder for herself. Annie Collins had asked off for yet another Friday night. Jessica had begrudgingly given the girl the night off, but she was also going to check the schedules for the past few months to see how often it was happening. And if it was as many times as she thought, she planned to sit the girl down and have a talk with her before her next shift.

"No."

Jessica snorted and tossed the pen down on the hostess podium as she looked at her boss over her shoulder. He eyed her silently as she put the cordless receiver back on the charging base and stepped away from the hostess stand to join him at the bar.

"No? You'd still have your name in there. But it might sound Christmasier. Kelley Green's Chop House."

"No," he repeated, deadpan.

"Then again, it might sound Irish." She slid onto a barstool and tipped her head to stare at Hayes Kelley.

"Who was that?" He nodded toward the phone on the hostess podium.

"Mm." Jessica squeezed her eyes closed and pinched the bridge of her nose. "Annie Collins. Asked off again for Friday."

"Which one is she?" Still with a straight face, Hayes shrugged.

"The blonde."

Hayes tipped his head and quirked an eyebrow at her. "Aren't there three or four blondes here now?"

Jessica laughed softly and dropped her hand to rest on the bar.

"They all look alike," Hayes mumbled as he turned his attention back to his notes.

"Women? Or just blondes?"

He grumbled something that Jessica didn't catch. She watched him for a moment as he worked through his menu plans for the coming week. Brow furrowed, eyes on his notes, Jessica knew she had lost him. Hayes Kelley was a tough nut to crack; she had known him since she had started waitressing for him her senior year of high school. Jessica supposed she had gotten to know him better than anyone else had in the past ten years, but that wasn't saying much.

In the scrappy t-shirts and flannels, the worn jeans, and the damned backwards ballcap, tourists probably thought Hayes Kelley was a janitor or fry cook. In reality, he was the owner of Kelley's Chop House and a renowned chef to boot. He was grumpy, but that grumpiness had grown on Jessica. She knew how to take him which was mostly with a grain of salt.

Her eighteen-year-old self had been scared of him when she first started waitressing for him. Hayes had been the manager then, not the owner. But as the restaurant manager, he had been her boss. After her third night working, a particularly bad night when a snippy older woman had read her the riot act for a menu change she'd had nothing to do with, Hayes had calmly explained to the customer the chef made those decisions, not the waitresses. Jessica had been a little bit in awe of the way he had the woman eating out of his hand before he walked away and a little bit irritated that the woman had been so predictable and warmed up to a good-looking guy talking to her.

She had been about to say as much to Hayes later in the evening when she clocked out. But he had given her a look—his eyes unexpectedly warm and friendly—and told her not to worry about women like Althea Gephart. That little olive branch had gone a long way toward soothing Jessica's anxiety and worry on the job and—probably to Hayes' dismay—to killing her fear of him.

"What do you think about blueberry peach pie?" he asked without looking up from his notes.

"In November?" She shook her head. "No."

"Why no?"

"Where're you gonna get peaches in November?"

"I can get 'em." He nodded.

"Do you need the extra expense?"

Hayes lifted his gaze to look at her. "I think so. Doesn't it sound good?"

Every damned pie Hayes made was good; Jessica figured if the guy made a traditional mud pie, it would somehow taste good. *Everything* he cooked tasted good. But she didn't want to admit that to him.

She shrugged. "I guess so?"

"Oh." He finally looked up and gave her a nod. "I get it."

Jessica narrowed her eyes at the smirk on his face.

"What? What do you get?"

"You don't wanna talk about peaches, do you?" The smirk blossomed into a full grin. Not only was Hayes really good in the kitchen, but he was also really good-looking. Sure, maybe she had to look harder some days, past the flannel and the grease-stained shirts, and the serious, unsmiling mug he always wore. But Hayes Kelley was sexy as hell.

"What does that mean?" She shook her head. Jesus, was he referring to her *boobs*? Didn't some guys refer to women's boobs as peaches? Hayes wasn't like that, though. In all the years she had known him, he had never made any inappropriate comments to her. Hell, in all the years she'd known him, she had never seen any indication that the guy had a *guy* brain. He never talked about women; Jessica only knew about his old engagement that crashed and burned and left him scarred and uninterested in pretty much *everything* *because* all of Holly Creek, New York, knew about it.

Broken engagement. He was young. She left him. Hayes retreated inside himself and never socialized. End of story. Apparently, it really was the end of the story, because Jessica had never heard another word about it.

"Umm." Hayes screwed his face up into a frown. "Let me think. Bourbon peach smash."

Stunned by his comment, Jessica could only stare at him, speechless.

"Ring a bell?" he asked innocently. "I mean, I guess I could see why you might object to peaches after that. But I thought it might be a fun change of pace from all the pumpkin and nutmeg this time of year."

He was talking about the party. Chelsea and Rex's big night. Chelsea's wedding was fast approaching, and all the wedding hoopla was beginning to make Jessica uncomfortable. If everything could have just been here in Holly Creek, she would be fine. She'd be *better* than fine, even with Rex's groomsmen. But she wasn't a big city person, and the idea of traveling to New York for her high school friend's wedding made her sick to her stomach.

Adding in the fact that she hadn't found a date yet, the stupid bet about finding their own dates, and the worry that Rex's mom might try to set her up with someone that weekend blew the roof off her anxiety.

Jessica dipped her head and laughed softly. "Who told you?"

"Who *didn't* tell me?" He reached for his glass of water and took a big drink. "Ran into Dee at the courthouse the other day. Saw Courtney at Brewed Awakening yesterday."

Jessica saw a chance to go on the offensive, so she took it.

"*You* were at Brewed Awakening? What in the world were you doing there?"

Hayes narrowed his eyes at her. "Getting coffee?"

"Not you." She shook her head. "You complain about spending ten bucks on a thirty-ounce store brand tub of ground coffee. I know you're not gonna pay for an overpriced fancy cup of coffee."

Jessica slipped off the stool and headed around the bar to go back to her office, eyes on Hayes as she went.

"I do not," he argued. "I just think it's worth it to clip coupons. I saved two bucks that time."

She chuckled. "And you're gonna do the extra spend for peaches in November?"

"I think I'm going to add a Bourbon Peach Smash to the cocktail list, too."

Jessica winced and shook her head.

"Rude."

"Courtney said something about turkey races." Hayes followed her to the office and leaned against the door frame when she sat down at her desk. Jessica tried to ignore him. She bumped the mouse and watched the desktop light up, unfortunately very aware of the smirk on Hayes' face.

"Might have been turkey races," she mumbled without looking at him.

"How'd you get so drunk?" He sounded genuinely curious. "I'm not sure I've ever seen you tipsy."

Jessica peeked at him but quickly jerked her gaze back to the computer. Using the mouse, she selected the previous month's payroll file and clicked on Annie Collins' name.

"Maybe because I don't usually drink much?"

"Yeah, I get that." He shrugged her question off. "You're a lightweight. But *why* did you drink so much? Knowing you're a lightweight?"

Jessica flopped back in the chair and eyed Hayes. He stared back boldly, waiting for her response.

She groaned and shrugged. "Because I don't love parties. And I don't like people."

Hayes crossed his arms over his chest and pursed his lips. "You love people."

"In my job, when I have to? To get a paycheck? Sure." She nodded. "But not really. And I really don't like Rex's groomsmen."

"Find a date yet?"

Why had she shared the details of that damned bet with Hayes Kelley? Sometimes, the guy was like a pain-in-the-ass older brother. He loved watching Jessica squirm.

"No."

"You're kinda runnin' out of time, Jess."

"I know." She nodded.

She was running out of time. Needing a date for a high society wedding in New York City was totally different than needing a date for a small-town wedding or other little community event here in Holly Creek.

"When's the last time you went out?"

"The party?" She looked at him with a frown and tossed her hands up in frustration.

"Doesn't count. I meant out on a date?"

"Why is that your concern?"

"I want my employees happy."

She snorted and rolled her eyes. "You can't even name two employees besides me."

His grin could get a girl in trouble. Good thing she wasn't interested in Hayes Kelley that way. Seemed like a good way to get her heart broken. He dropped his arms to his sides and stepped out of the doorway only to stick his head back in a second later.

"What is a turkey race, anyway? What does that entail?"

Jessica laughed, but she grabbed a pad of sticky notes and threw it at him.

"Hey. No violence in the workplace!" he called. Jessica could hear him laughing as he walked away.

CHAPTER 2

*H*ayes

Not quite satisfied with the new menu items, Hayes returned to his notes at the bar and left Jessica alone. As much as he liked teasing her, she had work to do, and he still had a hundred things on his to-do list before they opened tonight. Wondering what time it was, he patted his pockets down for his phone. He hated the damned thing and rarely used it for anything other than telling the time. Realizing he must have left it in the kitchen, he grunted his frustration and went back to his notes.

He had a meeting with Sean Wallace sometime this afternoon. Having a local beer on tap was a no-brainer for any restaurant, but Sean's and Jax Bigsley's Harvest Hues Amber Ale had sold out faster than anything else Hayes ever had on tap. The new holiday brew was popular, but stouts in general weren't as popular as amber ales. Hayes was still anxious to get more of the Cocoa Noel Stout on order—the ridiculous holiday name made him cringe—and talk to Sean about what the new year would bring.

Hayes flinched when the upbeat music started playing around him. Jessica had apparently turned the speakers on. Fine with him; they always played something for background music, usually instrumental soft rock or jazz. This was neither. Hayes leaned forward to rest his elbows on the bar and covered his ears as some woman sang about a Santa Train. The vocal *hoo-hoos* made him cringe. The fiddle made him want to crawl under the bar and hide.

"What is this torture?" he called to Jessica. Assuming his complaint would fall on deaf ears, Hayes lifted his head and went back to work. He jotted down a note for sweet potato gratin, whipped feta roast potatoes, and fall salads. Last year his Fall Harvest salad had been a big hit. He had been debating trying a Farro salad. Or maybe he should double down on soup ideas since the winter months were coming.

Jessica's laughter preceded her. Hayes looked over his shoulder as she pushed through the swinging kitchen doors. She carried a calendar with her, and the severe look on her face indicated she intended to do some real business now.

"Christmas music," she answered without looking at him. She sidled up to the bar right beside him and put the calendar down.

"No shit, Jess." He rolled his eyes. "Who is it?"

"Patty Loveless."

"And she is?"

"A country music star popular in the late eighties and nineties." She smoothed her hand over the calendar and looked up at him.

"And what? She's your favorite? No, wait." He turned sideways and leaned into the bar. "Your parents saw her in concert—"

"No. And no." She shook her head with a frown. "Look at this—"

"Then why are we listening to her?"

"Well, we're not now." She shrugged.

Hayes tipped his chin up and realized the song had changed to "Marshmallow World." He didn't recognize this singer's voice either. It wasn't Patty Loveless, though. No fiddles or banjos. But it wasn't Dean Martin, either.

"So, Ann—"

"Why are we listening to Christmas music?" He cut her off. When Jessica had first started waitressing here, she was young and timid. Afraid of him, nervous around their customers, Hayes didn't think she would last a week. Ten years later, the steakhouse was his, she was his restaurant manager, she was incredible with their customers and employees, and if she took shit from him, she gave it right back.

Hayes loved sparring with her. He loved that flicker of annoyance that she used to try to hide from him. He loved it when he said something ridiculous to exasperate her. He loved it when he made her laugh. While he wasn't interested in women or love or dating ever again, Jessica Bradshaw was at the top of his list of favorite humans.

"Because it's Christmas time, Hayes." She sighed.

"It's still November."

"Most people start decorating in November. People shop all year now. It's a thing." She gave him a shrug. "Last Friday was Black Friday. It's happening, Hayes. Get used to it."

"I hate Christmas music," he grumbled.

He didn't.

Well, not *all* of it.

But Jessica loved it, therefore he enjoyed pretending to hate it.

"Can we talk for a minute?" She arched her brows and tipped her head.

Hayes studied her with a frown. He had assumed she had something work-related to talk about. But what if...

He glanced at the calendar and back at her. Had she asked anyone to go to the wedding with her? Hell, Hayes knew Chelsea, too. Wasn't close to her like Jessica was, but Chelsea was a Holly Creek girl, therefore he *knew* her. But he hated weddings. Especially big frilly fancy weddings. And he knew without a doubt that Chelsea's big city wedding would be a fancy pain-in-the-ass.

"No." He shook his head and turned back to his menu notes. Time to quit jacking around. He still had no idea what time it was, but Sean would probably be here soon. He should have asked if he could come down to the brewery. A trip to the brewery would serve two purposes—it would get him away from the holiday music, away from any possible chance Jessica had to ask him to go with her to the wedding, and if Sean and Jax had anything new going, he would most likely get to taste it.

"No?" she snapped. "What do you mean no?"

"Ask someone else."

"Hayes."

"I hate weddings. I hate couples. I hate New York. I don't do monkey suits. And I don't dance."

Jessica narrowed her eyes at him for a moment and then burst into a loud, hearty belly laugh.

"What?" He folded his arms over his chest again.

"You thought—?" She snorted and dabbed at her eyes. "God. No."

"No?"

"No." She shook her head, rubbed gently at her eyes, and finally met his gaze again. "No. I'm not asking you to go to the wedding with me."

For a half a second, Hayes was terrified. Terrified his mouth would blurt out something completely asinine. Like *why wouldn't you ask me to go with you to the wedding? Why am I not wedding date material in your mind?*

Thankfully, that half a second passed, and he was thrilled knowing she hadn't even considered it. He liked her. They had fun together. *Here.* Getting ready for a work night. They worked well together. They had drinks now and then after hours. Hell, they'd hung out a few times around town, always with other people around, and had a good time.

But no. The wedding thing would be a terrible idea. He was glad she thought so, too.

Wasn't he?

"Then, what? I have a meeting with Sean Wallace this afternoon."

"Oh, yeah." She wagged her eyebrows. "Forgot about that."

"No. You do not need to be part of the meeting."

"I might." She argued.

"I thought you had a thing for Jax."

"I don't have a thing for either of them." She rolled her eyes. "They're just fun to look at."

"Wow. And women complain about men objectifying them."

Jessica closed her eyes and shook her head. "I didn't say they have nice asses. I said they're fun to look at."

"You didn't say that they're nice guys or make really good beer, though."

"They do make good beer," she agreed. "Annie. Look at this." She flattened her hand on the calendar as she turned away from him. "She's asked off four of the last seven Fridays. And she's called in three times."

Hayes studied the calendar, Jessica's efficient, easily legible handwriting all over it. Annie Collins had indeed missed too much work. She'd only been here seven months; he had plenty of employees who had been with him for years—Jessica included—who deserved weekends off and never got them.

"Remind me again." He drummed his fingers on the bar. Christmas music still played; he liked the current song. Odds were he had heard it before, but it wasn't a classic holiday tune.

"Blonde."

"Bradshaw." He sighed when she laughed softly.

"Wears her hair in the bun. Has a tattoo of Curious George on her left arm."

"That's Annie?" Totally not the blonde he had been picturing.

"She's single."

"Have you talked to her about it yet?"

"No."

"One warning," he told Jessica.

"I'll talk to her before her next shift."

CHAPTER 3

*J*essica

While Jessica didn't mind looking at Sean Wallace or his business partner, Jax, she didn't have any crazy designs on either of them. Jax and Dee had dated and broken up a few times, anyway. Besides, she wasn't looking for a guy. She just needed a date for Chelsea's damned wedding.

Reminded of the wedding, she sat back in her chair and thought about Hayes. His preemptive no about being her wedding date. Even now, the whole idea made her laugh. She would have as much fun at a weekend wedding with *Oscar the Grouch*. At least Hayes would be more fun to look at.

Satisfied that she had the schedule set for the coming week, Jessica left her office in search of Jonah Larson. One of the line cooks, he had burned his arm the week before on French fry grease. The ER doctor had treated him for third degree burns. Jessica wasn't convinced he needed to be back at work yet, and she was certain she had heard his voice a few minutes ago.

She wandered through the kitchen, talking with a few other employees, but not seeing Jonah. Two of their wait staff danced in the hall outside the kitchen to "Have Yourself a Merry Little Christmas." Jessica offered them a big smile and a thumbs up as she passed on through to go to the bar.

The holidays made Hayes crazy. He had rolled his eyes dramatically when she and Capri, another waitress, had decorated the tree last week, before Thanksgiving. Before the damned party where she had indeed had way too much to drink. But Jessica loved everything about Christmas. Maybe she wasn't as bad as Chelsea—she wouldn't plan a Christmas wedding with all the red and green. But she couldn't help but feel a little spring in her step now.

As she pushed through the swinging doors to the bar again, she heard male voices. She stifled a laugh; she'd managed to venture out in time to see Sean even if she had only been joking with Hayes earlier.

"Hey." Sean nodded as she joined Hayes behind the bar.

"Hey." She stood beside Hayes again. "How's it going?"

"Sounds like it's going pretty well," Sean told her. "Hayes says the Cocoa Noel isn't quite as popular as the Harvest Hues Amber Ale. But it's doing pretty good."

"A lot of our patrons don't like the heavier beers," she answered with a shrug.

"You liked it, didn't you?"

"I did." She nodded, aware of the smirk on Hayes' face as he watched her talking to Sean. "I'd drink one right now, but my boss doesn't allow me to drink on the job."

"Bullshit." Hayes coughed and covered his mouth.

She and Sean shared a grin.

"I thought I heard Jonah's voice." Jessica glanced at Hayes.

"You did." Hayes nodded. "He came in to talk to you for a minute."

"Okay." She looked around. "Where'd he go?"

"Talked to me instead."

"Why would he do that?"

"I dunno," Hayes answered with a dramatic shrug. "Maybe because I'm better-looking than you."

Jessica snorted. "Right."

"I'm gonna have to beg to differ," Sean announced.

"He said his doctor cleared him to come back to work, but he promised his parents he would help them with Christmas lights. So he was hoping for another day off."

"I don't have him on the schedule until Friday."

"Perfect." Hayes nodded.

"Get a date for the wedding yet?"

"Jesus," Jessica mumbled. She narrowed her eyes at Sean and sighed. "You, too?"

"What?" He shrugged innocently. "Just asking. I'll be there."

"Really?"

"Don't do it, man. Weddings give me the creeps." Hayes shuddered as he pulled a pint of the Cocoa Noel stout from the tap.

"I don't let him out much. He doesn't know how to socialize," Jessica said to Sean.

"Speaking of which—"

"No." Hayes cut him off.

"Poker game. Sunday night."

Jessica watched Hayes eye Sean with interest.

"Your place?"

"Nah. Andrew O'Shea's house."

"Nice." Hayes nodded.

"You play poker?" Jessica asked him, unable to hide her surprise.

"I do." He nodded again. He lifted the pint glass and took a drink. "This would be better with some cookies."

"Dude." Jessica rolled her eyes. "Beer and cookies don't mix."

"Beer mixes with anything," Sean corrected her. "Even a hangover."

"Here we go." She dropped her head back and closed her eyes. "Just hit me. Get it over with."

"I'd never hit a lady," Sean argued. "I'd be a real peach if I did that."

Jessica cracked a smile when Hayes and Sean roared with laughter.

"Court said you don't like Rex's groomsmen."

She shrugged a shoulder. "None of us are too crazy about his groomsmen."

"She also said you lost a shoe."

"What?"

"At the party. You lost a shoe."

Hayes snorted and took another drink.

"I did not lose a shoe," Jessica corrected Sean. "I took my shoes off and carried them from one bar to another, because they were killing me."

"Shouldn't wear 'em."

"Shoes?" She glanced at Hayes with a frown.

"Heels."

"They were flats."

"Hmm." He handed her the pint glass, now half full. "Have a beer. You seem a little tense."

The smell of the beer made her feel slightly queasy. It had been a few days; she should be over this hangover from hell by now. Knowing Hayes and Sean were both watching her, expecting her to shy away from any alcohol because of the hangover she'd had, she took a drink and swallowed with ease.

"Blue Crawford's probably free."

"For what?" Jessica put the glass down, folded her arms on the bar, and looked at Sean expectantly.

"The wedding."

Blue Crawford was a recluse. Not terribly bad-looking. And polite enough if she happened to run into him, which as far as she could remember was three times in the fourteen years she had lived in Holly Creek. But the man only ventured out to the grocery store a few times a year. No way in hell he would know who she was, let alone want to go to the city with her.

Not that she would ask him.

"I think I'm gonna pass," she told Sean. "I'll figure it out."

She took the stout beer with her back to her office and plopped into her desk chair. After another drink of the beer, she decided Hayes might be right. The Cocoa Noel stout might be okay with a chocolate cookie of some sort. Maybe a fudge brownie cookie.

For now, she had other things to think about.

Like the wedding. She needed a date.

Time was ticking, and she was no closer to figuring it out than she had been at the engagement party in July when this whole bet got started.

CHAPTER 4

*H*ayes

He liked nature. Woodlands. Mountains. Beaches, though like any other guy, he liked the beaches more for the women who chose to sunbathe there. Preferably topless. At night, after the kitchen closed, sometimes if the bar was busy, he would help up front and then come out back where he liked to sit and star gaze. Savor a pour of bourbon.

In the summer, he could and had sat out back damned near all night long. On more than one occasion. In the winter, he would still sit outside—relaxing and cooling off after a frantic night in the kitchen. Tonight, a million stars lit up the midnight sky. Reason number one why he would never live in a big city. He would much rather see the skies, the stars or clouds, than look at skyscrapers.

Jessica had toned the Christmas music down a bit for the dinner hours. Something a little jazzy, but all instrumental. All played low enough to be background music, nothing to interfere with a date night or family conversations.

Annie had worked tonight. He had seen the girl come in

and sneak through the kitchen, as if she knew she was in for an ass-chewing. She was lucky it was Jessica that sat down with her. True, even when he was angry, Hayes was pretty mellow. But odds were he would have fired her tonight. With Jessica, at least she would get one more chance.

He didn't flinch when he heard the back door open behind him. Probably Jessica. He shifted on the picnic table, patted his pockets, only to come up empty again.

"What time is it?" he asked without looking to see for sure it was Jessica.

"Ten after." She dropped to sit by him on the table. "Everybody's out. Hampton's on clean up."

Hampton was the best bartender Hayes had ever seen. The guy was quick with his hands, quick to recognize anyone who bellied up to his bar, and quick with a joke or a quirky comeback when one was called for.

"Good."

"It was a good night," she announced. Hayes glanced at her.

"You sound surprised."

"Early in the week." She shrugged.

"Holiday season," he reminded her.

She snickered as she looked at him. "Now you're gonna play the holiday card?"

Hayes simply stared at her, knowing the intense look didn't bother her anymore. Rather than comment, she reached over, cupped her hand around his fist, and uncurled his fingers. Hayes held his breath while she stared at the unlit cigarette.

"How long are you gonna do this?" she asked quietly.

Her gentle tone grated on his nerves. He had no answer. Simply shrugged. He'd been a smoker in high school. Quit when he started dating Lisa. And started again when she left. Four years later, his dad had been diagnosed with emphysema and asked him to quit. A smoker for life, Wilson Kelley had finally quit just before his diagnosis. Hayes hadn't really given a rat's ass about his own health at the time, but he hadn't wanted to cause his dad any stress. So he quit a second time.

But he still sat out back here every night after the Chop House closed and held an unlit cigarette until the urge to light it up left him alone. For the night. He wasn't sure he would ever *not* want to light it.

"Long as it takes, huh?"

Hayes felt Jessica's sigh as much as he heard it.

"The mayor was in tonight," she told him.

"Yeah?" That surprised him. Ezekiel usually made his presence known to Hayes or ducked into the kitchen for a minute to say hello.

"Had a high school kid ask me—"

"Out?"

"No." She rolled her eyes. "Why I didn't have the same accent as most everyone around here."

Hayes laughed quietly. Jessica had been raised in the Midwest. Her family had moved to Holly Creek when she was starting her freshman year of high school. Like Hayes—also a transplant from a different area in the Midwest—she had never acquired the New York accent.

"So do Sean and Jax have something new going?"

Hayes nodded. "Didn't say what yet. Told me they'd give me a call next week at the latest."

"How's Wilson doing?"

"Cantankerous as always," Hayes answered. He hated talking about his family. Himself. His past. But Jessica had broken down that wall a while ago, at least a few years ago. Hayes had to juggle a family emergency—Wilson had a heart attack—with getting to the Chop House to get the night going. When Jessica found out how thin he had stretched himself that night, she lit into him about delegating and sharing the responsibilities. Hayes still wasn't good at delegating, but he was getting better. It helped that Jessica could do just about anything he could at the Chop House.

Except cook.

He'd watched her burn a grilled cheese sandwich once. When she was standing right over the stovetop.

"Did he finish his antibiotics?"

His dad had come down with pneumonia just before Thanksgiving. Hayes had dragged his dad out of the house, to his truck, and driven him to see Dr. Addison. Naturally, Wilson hadn't believed the doctor when he said it was pneumonia, even though the old man was so congested he couldn't breathe and nearly coughed up a lung anytime he opened his mouth. According to Wilson Kelley, Dr. Addison was just a smartass young whipper snapper who was too big for his britches.

Which Hayes found interesting, given that his dad was in his late sixties. The way he talked, a person might believe he was in his nineties.

"I think so." Hayes shrugged. Since Wilson didn't believe he had pneumonia, Hayes had had a hell of a time getting the man to take his antibiotic.

Hayes had heard the saying about someone rolling over in his grave, but he figured his mother was dancing, maybe *laughing*, in her grave. Hayes had been a pain-in-the-ass kid. All boy. Mouthy and always into something. He had loved his mom more than anything, but he'd put his parents through a lot of shit when he was a kid. She probably thought it was karma that Hayes was now dealing with his stubborn dad.

"My dad was looking at motorcycles over the weekend."

"Yeah?" Hayes looked at Jessica curiously. He had been around her parents enough to know that her mom wasn't about to let her dad buy a motorcycle. "How'd that go over?"

She laughed and shook her head. "She told him she'd divorce him before he spilled his gray matter on the road, and she became his caretaker instead of his wife."

"That shit happens," he mumbled. He knew someone from school who had messed up his back and ribs in a bike accident.

"I know. I think Dad's just looking at them because my sister's boyfriend has one."

"Yeah, I can't believe your mom is letting her date him."

"Amelia's twenty-five, Hayes. She stopped listening to them when she was seventeen."

Hayes shrugged. "Your mom told you to stop going out with Mark Holt."

"I didn't, though," she answered and continued when Hayes gave her a look to call her on her bullshit, "not right away."

He harrumphed, wishing he'd brought himself a pour of bourbon out with him. The adrenaline rush from the night was fading, and the cold was beginning to get to him.

"Besides, she was right." Jessica leaned forward and rested her elbows on her knees. "Mark was—"

"An asshat," Hayes finished for her. Hayes wasn't sure he'd liked any of the guys Jessica had gone out with, but Mark topped the list of asshats.

"True." She sighed now and tipped her head forward to rub her neck. Hayes watched her for a moment, her long, slender fingers working the long column of her neck. In the tiny floodlight out here behind the Chop House, her skin had a yellow cast to it.

"What's wrong?"

"Amelia just texted me an hour ago," she answered as she straightened. "They're going to Cancun after Christmas."

"She and Nolan?"

"Yep."

Hayes had met Amelia's boyfriend, too. The guy was probably his age, a good nine or ten years older than Jessica's sister. He was divorced with a kid that he rarely saw, but Hayes didn't know the whole story. It was possible Nolan didn't want to see the kid, but also possible the ex had full custody and made it difficult for Nolan to see him. Hayes knew exactly what he was getting out of dating Jessica's sister, but he couldn't figure out what she liked about it.

Well. Other than the money he threw around.

"And I can't find a date for one event."

"You haven't looked," he argued.

"Have to." She straightened and looked at him. "I asked a couple of guys I went to school with. One has a girlfriend. The other moved to San Diego."

"That's two guys."

"I asked Stirling to go with me," she reminded him. "And he said yes. Now he can't. Something came up."

"Stirling Roberts is gay."

"Rex's mother doesn't know that."

"Well, she would after taking one look." Hayes drilled her with a *get-real* look.

Jessica snorted and shook her head.

"Doesn't matter anyway," she mumbled. "I got dumped by my gay friend."

"Isn't he going home for Christmas? For his grandma's birthday?"

"Yep."

"Hardly dumped you. And you can do better."

"I don't need to do better.," she argued. "Stirling's a safe date."

Hayes understood needing a safe date. Just a plus one for an event as opposed to a person to be in a relationship with. But he didn't get why Jessica would prefer a safe date.

"Who's next on your list?"

"I dunno." She took a deep breath. "Maybe I'll get my cousin to fly up and go with me."

"Eww." Hayes shuddered. "Gross. Think harder."

She slid off the table and stood for a moment looking at the sky.

"Looking for Santa or wishing on a star?"

She flashed him a grin over her shoulder. "I think I'm a little too old for either."

CHAPTER 5

*J*essica

Mornings should have been hard with the hours she kept. They weren't, though. Jessica was up, sipping coffee at the bistro table in her tiny kitchen by eight. She hadn't showered yet, but she had nowhere to go for a while. Slow start mornings were nice; she used to roll her eyes at her parents when they said so. But now she understood.

Not that she would tell them that. At twenty-eight, Jessica had started to see the world, life, through her parents' eyes. She understood the value of money and hard work, when maybe at sixteen and eighteen she didn't fully grasp the concepts. She loved her job, loved working for Hayes, even on his grouchy days, and she enjoyed meeting new people when she wandered through the dining area in the Chop House. Her parents used to tell her she needed a job that satisfied her, that gave her a purpose. If she let on now that she did, that she agreed with what they said, if she hinted that she loved slow start mornings or that she hated how fast the years were flying by, they would preen, proud of themselves for their wisdom.

And yes, they would probably remind her that they had told her so.

All in fun, of course. Jessica had to roll her eyes at her parents from time to time, but they were close. Even though her parents tended to give her sister more leeway than they'd ever given Jessica, they were a close family.

When she was a kid, her parents would start weekend mornings with coffee and the news in bed. That or a huge breakfast, both still in their pjs, cooking together, sipping their coffee, and talking. They were affectionate with each other, always had been. She and Amelia had played and watched cartoons until they were older and grossed out by their parents' shows of affection.

Now, Jessica liked that they were still all googly-eyed at each other all the time. And she wanted the same for her sister and herself. Kind of sucked that her kid sister was being pampered with money and attention and probably incredible sex when Jessica hadn't had any of the above in what seemed like forever. But she could deal with it if she liked Nolan. And she might like Nolan if he weren't ten years older than Amelia. And divorced. With a kid he didn't seem too into.

She worried about her sister, that was all. They were friends, had always had a good relationship, and Jessica wouldn't waste time being jealous of her if she thought Nolan was good for her. Not that she was really jealous.

In fact, all she needed right now was a date. For *one* weekend. Just a friend. It wasn't like Jessica was looking for a relationship—well, not like she expected this glamorous, weekend wedding date to be the beginning of anything. The problem was Holly Creek was a small town. She knew most people who lived here, and she had asked her three male friends—one of them being Stirling. One was across the country, and the other two had both said they would go with her if they could, but both had plans and couldn't make it. Which left Jessica back at the drawing board.

She put her phone down when she heard the knock on her front door. Barefoot, she padded through the short hall to her cozy living room and pulled the door open. Shocked to find Hayes Kelley on the stoop, she blinked at him silently. Behind him, the sky was a shade lighter than steel gray; the clouds hanging heavy, as if it might snow at any moment. She was ready for it. She didn't love snow, but she would rather look at a snow-covered yard than dead, dry grass. Once the trees lost their fall-colored leaves, they looked better coated in snow, too.

"What're—pajamas?" Hayes waved his hand at her, his face twisted in a mask of confusion. "Wake up, Bradshaw."

"I'm—" Jessica decided against arguing with him and clamped her mouth shut.

Hayes looked over his shoulder and back to her. "You gonna let me in?"

Still flustered to find her boss at her front door, Jessica gave herself a mental shake and stepped aside to let him in.

"What're you doing here?" She pushed the door closed, crossed her arms over her chest, and shivered.

"I got ambushed at Brewed Awakening," he grumbled and waved the white wax bag at her. "Do I smell coffee?"

Jessica narrowed her eyes at him and finally shook her head. "What?"

"Get some clothes on, Bradshaw," he told her as he turned and headed toward her kitchen. He had never been to her house, but then, it was small enough that he knew if the kitchen wasn't at the front of the house, it had to be at the end of the hall.

"I have clothes on," she mumbled as she finally stirred and followed. She heard her phone buzzing as she walked down the hall behind him. Hayes leaned over the island to look at her phone as he put the Brewed Awakening bag down.

"It's your mom."

"Gee, thanks." She snatched the phone and stabbed the screen so hard, she was surprised she didn't break a nail. "Hey, Mom."

"Hi, Jess. Busy?"

"Not at all," she answered, eyes on Hayes. He rolled his, confirming what Jessica suspected. Not only did he know who had called her, he could hear the other end of the conversation.

"Dad and I are taking Amelia and Nolan to dinner Saturday. Can you go?"

"Working." It was probably wrong for her to feel the level of relief she did. She did *not* want to go to dinner with Amelia and Nolan. Jessica stepped closer to the counter and reached for the coffee pot.

"What if we changed it to brunch Sunday?"

"Busy." She jerked her gaze up to look at Hayes.

"Doing what?"

Hayes arched his eyebrows at her mom's question.

"Working."

"You're not open for brunch. The Chop House isn't open at all on Sundays," her mom reminded her.

"I'm helping Hayes with inventory."

"Inventory of what?" Of course her mom knew she was making excuses. The last time her mom called with the same invitation, Jessica had begged off saying she was coming down with something.

Eyes locked with Hayes' now, Jessica bit her lip and sighed as quietly as possible.

"Food, Mom," she said simply. "Somebody has to count the eggs now and then."

Hayes gave her a frown, so she turned away from him, still holding the pot of coffee in her right hand.

"He's not going anywhere, Jess." Her mom's gentle tone made her bristle. How did her parents like Nolan Barrett?

"I'll talk to Hayes," Jessica mumbled. "See if I can get out of inventory."

Even plagued with guilt for repeatedly dodging the dinner invitation, she couldn't bring herself to just agree to go with them.

"Okay. Call me back." As if her mom bought it. Jessica stifled another sigh and said goodbye. She tapped her screen to end the call, put her phone on the counter, and took another cup from the cabinet to the right of the sink.

"What was that all about?" Hayes asked when she turned back to him and put the empty cup on the island.

"You know what that was about, so don't pretend like you don't." She eyed him warily. "What are you doing here?"

"Told you." He kept his eyes on the brown liquid as she poured the cup full. "Got—"

"Nope." She shook her head and refilled her cup. "First of all. Brewed Awakening again? What gives, Hayes?"

"Nothing."

"Liar." She returned the pot to the burner and slid onto her stool again. "I think you've got a thing for Sabs. She's super cute, but I didn't realize blue hair was your type."

"I do. Not. Have a thing for Sabrina." He spoke in a monotone.

Jessica loved Sabrina; the snarky blue-haired girl was her hero. She loved the quiet sarcasm, the way people who didn't know her well assumed she was shy. Jessica knew, too, that

Hayes didn't have a thing for her. They were friendly. End of story.

Fun to rib him, though.

"Why, if you were just at Brewed Awakening, are you here? Drinking my coffee?"

"Who says I didn't have coffee there, too?"

She eyed him quietly for a moment and finally nodded. "Yeah, you do look a little on edge. Not sure you need the caffeine."

"Please." Another grumble.

Hayes Kelley existed on caffeine. Specifically black coffee.

"You have five minutes." She ducked her head and scrubbed her fingers back through her hair.

"Or what? Your scrawny self is gonna throw me out?"

"Yes." She nodded and snapped her fingers at him.

"I've been going to Brewed Awakening because I heard that there's some new business guy thinking about coming to town."

"Who?"

Hayes shrugged. "No idea. But I've heard he's linked to big businesses. Like chains."

"Chain restaurants?" She tipped her head.

"No, but if we end up with a box store or two here, what's stopping all the chain restaurants from coming, too?"

He had a point. "So, you're hanging out there to eavesdrop."

"Yep."

"Because that's not suspicious at all. Hayes Kelley, local anti-social cheapskate, hanging out at a trendy coffee shop?"

"Ouch." He patted his hand over his heart. "You really know how to hurt a guy."

"Right." She nodded. "First, if you want to eavesdrop, I

would start at the diner. Second. Yeah, okay, definitely worthwhile to eavesdrop in this situation."

"See." He pointed at her, took a drink, and set his cup down.

"Still doesn't explain why you're *here*."

"Ambushed," he reminded her. Jessica stared at him blankly and finally shrugged.

"What does that mean?"

"Samantha Reed and Lila Anderson cornered me."

"Lila Anderson, Dr. Anderson's wife?"

"Yes."

"About what?"

Why would the two of them corner Hayes? Sure, Samantha Reed was heavily involved in community improvement. As a small business owner herself, the owner of a salon, Samantha might have knowledge about big businesses butting their way into Holly Creek's commerce, but what did Lila have to do with it?

"You."

"Me?" Jessica yelped. "What?"

"They gave me a list of men for you to consider for the bet."

"They *what*?" She jumped off her stool, mad enough she thought steam might be shooting from her ears. "What the hell, Hayes? Why is this everyone's business?"

"Because they didn't love the mother-of-the-groom. She made her rounds, ya know? When she was here for the engagement party? They don't want her struttin' around come wedding weekend when you show up without a date."

Speechless, Jessica narrowed her eyes at him. "I can get a date."

"Well, just in case. They sent me here with breakfast and a list. No one minds making a donation to charity, and apparently, most people kind of like the chicken dance—"

"For fuck's sake." She groaned as she lifted her hands to rub her temples.

"I personally think the chicken dance is the dumbest thing ever to exist," he continued, "but I have to admit, I'm not crazy about Rex's mom, either. So. Here I am."

Jessica sighed and leaned over to rest her elbows on the island.

"I feel like freaking Cinderella. Like you're my fairy godfather here to set me up in style for the wedding weekend."

"I am not a fairy anything, thank you very much. But Samantha and Lila insisted, and frankly, I'm ready for your date issue to be solved. So let's sit down and figure it out."

CHAPTER 6

*H*ayes

When he was a kid, maybe eleven or twelve, he and his friends snuck lingerie catalogs from their parents' mail so they could check out the models. They had been too young, obviously, because half the contraptions the models wore made no sense to them. But as he got older, Hayes developed an appreciation for silk and lace. Straps. Garters. Skin. Breasts. Nipples. Hell, he could never have been just a boob guy or a butt guy. He loved it all.

And then Lisa happened, and maybe a few pointless, go-nowhere one-night stands, and now here he was looking at Jessica in fleece pj pants and an oversized, worn sweatshirt, and something weird was going on in his gut.

Jessica.

For fuck's sake. She had worked for him for ten years now. She was a *kid.*

Except she wasn't. Not anymore. She had been a scrawny runt when he hired her. Cute, but she had never registered on his radar then. Because she was young and because he was still wallowing in the dregs of heartbreak.

Jessica had changed. Hayes wasn't blind; she was a beautiful woman, and he had noticed the changes as they happened. She'd filled out, had curves in all the right places. A kid had gone off to college, and a woman had come back in her place. She'd cut her long dark hair. It had grown some, but she kept it just a bit past her shoulders now. She dressed professionally—slacks and feminine blouses or sweaters. She was good for his business, the perfect face and personality forward to meet their diners each night.

Hayes saw her in ripped up jeans and sweatshirts and shorts now and then. Holly Creek was too small not to run into people when he was out and about. But he'd never seen her in pajamas, and even though the fleece pants with Christmas llamas on them were a far cry from the sexy things he had peeled off women through the years, his dick had decided this was a good moment to stir and make its presence known.

"I don't need your help." She shook her head.

"Blue Crawford made their list," he ignored her as he pulled a folded slip of paper from his back pocket. "So, maybe he *is* someone you should consider. Sean might know him, and if Lila and Samantha think he's good—"

"This is not happening."

To Hayes' dismay, Jessica tugged her sweatshirt off and tossed it aside on the counter. By the toaster. The silver Black and Decker toaster. The one he didn't dare look away from since his employee was now standing in her kitchen topless.

"The hell are you doing?" he snapped. His eyes wanted to jerk that way. To look at her. What hot-blooded American male wouldn't want to look at a topless Jessica Bradshaw? Hell, *any* topless woman?

"You're making me hot." Her tone was heavy with irritation, not lust, thank God.

He grunted in response. From the corner of his eye, he saw her lift her hands and drag them through her hair. *He* was making her hot? His blood pressure was probably dangerously close to blowing the top off his head. Or maybe some other disaster a little further south on his body.

A peel of laughter jerked his gaze to her. She stared at him with bright green eyes, her lips tipped up in a genuine smile. He blinked, let his eyes roam only to find that she was not topless. She had a navy thermal tee on. No wonder she was hot.

"What's so funny?"

"You panicked, didn't you?" she snorted. "Did you really think I was going to whip my top off like that in front of you?"

"You did whip your top off," he reminded her. Suddenly sweating under his flannel shirt, he shrugged out of it and dropped it over his lap. "Can we get back to this list?"

"If that means I get rid of you sooner, yes, let's get back to the list."

She scooted her stool closer to him. Hayes drew back when her scent hit him. Perfume or soap or lotion. He smelled it on her every day at the Chop House, but somehow it was different here in her kitchen.

"So, for starters." She tugged the list away from him and smoothed the paper flat on the island. Her natural nails were short but perfectly rounded in shape. No polish. He had never seen Jessica wear any nail polish. She wore a ring with a little red stone on the middle finger of her right hand. He had no idea who it was from, what it symbolized, if anything. Only that she'd begun wearing it when she was away at college. "I'm not going to ask Blue Crawford to go with me to the wedding. So we can mark him off."

"I think you should consider it."

"Why?" She tipped her chin up to eye him with a frown. "No. End of story."

"You don't have to sleep with him. You know that, right?"

"What?" She slipped off the chair backwards and turned her back to him. "Seriously, Hayes?"

"I mean, you're not thinking that, right? You don't owe anyone sex for going with you to this wedding."

She opened a drawer, snatched something from it, slammed it closed again, and turned back to him. Clicking a pen in her hand, she shot him another severe frown.

"No, I'm not thinking that. I asked Stirling, remember?"

"Yeah, but I mean, if Blue took you or if that guy you dated in high school took you, you don't owe anyone that kind of thank you."

Hayes almost squirmed under her heavy stare. Why was he hammering her on this particular point? Yes, he absolutely believed Jessica didn't owe any guy a sexual payback for being her date for the wedding. He would believe that no matter who he was talking to, never mind that she was his employee. His friend.

"Yeah. Got it." She nodded and looked back at the paper again.

Hayes hated the thought of her with Blue Crawford. Or Stirling. Or Sean. Or anyone. Not just the sex part. He didn't make a habit of thinking of his employees that way. But Jessica didn't adjust well in crowds of people. She normally handled it well; and she would no doubt fool anyone at the wedding. But her anxiety would be astronomical that whole weekend.

He didn't like thinking that she would be that uncomfortable when she was gone.

That's what he told himself, anyway.

He watched her scratch off another few names. Four more. Six more. Until there were no names left.

"Yeah, thanks." She clicked the pen and crumbled the paper up to throw it away. "Look, if I don't get a date, I'll deal with it."

"If any video surfaces of you doing the chicken dance at a high society wedding in New York, I might have to fire you."

The tension broke, and Jessica laughed out loud just as someone knocked on her door.

"Wow. Busy place today," she mumbled.

"Want me to leave?"

"No." She headed down the hall to the front of the house again. Hayes' stomach growled, so he reached for the bag from Brewed Awakening. Might as well eat the pastry he'd brought.

"Hey."

He hesitated, pastry en route to his mouth, when he heard Jessica greet whoever was at her door. Cold air blasted through the small house, cooling his bare arms. Now that she was out of the room, the idea that Jessica Bradshaw could turn him on was laughable. For fuck's sake. He didn't even do porn anymore.

Nothing. Nada. No girlfriend. No flings. No porn.

And he was just thirty-five.

What the—

"Hi. Mom called." Amelia's voice carried down the hall to him.

"Great."

Hayes recognized the sarcasm in Jessica's voice.

"Got a minute?"

Apparently, Amelia didn't hear the sarcasm. Either that, or she didn't care.

"Not really, no." Jessica's voice grew closer. Hayes looked up to find Amelia staring at him in surprise. *Oh boy*. This didn't look good. It was early for restaurant people. And Jessica was in pjs. Which her sister undoubtedly recognized as pjs. Amelia might not alert the gossips in town, but she would surely rib the shit out of Jess. And she would damned well be sure to tell their parents she had found Hayes at Jess' place.

"Hi, Hayes." She turned immediately to the counter to eye the coffee pot. Either deciding there wasn't enough, or she didn't want any, she moved on to the refrigerator and took a canned soda out.

"Gross," Jessica hissed as she popped the top.

"What're you doing here?" Amelia leaned on the counter at her back and stared boldly at him.

"Talking shop," Jessica answered before he could say a word. Without even a glance in her direction, Hayes nodded.

"Really."

From her tone, Hayes assumed Amelia didn't believe them. But she turned to Jessica without further comment.

"So. Really? You've turned Mom down six times now. To have dinner with me and Nolan."

"It hasn't been six times." Jessica's attempt at arguing was feeble at best. Hayes flinched. It bothered Jessica that her little sister was involved with someone, and she couldn't get a date for one weekend. It was more than that, and he knew it, even if they didn't talk about it often. But Jessica didn't like Nolan, and it bugged her that her parents did.

"It has," Amelia told her with a nod. "She's marking each time on her calendar. I've seen it. Today was number six."

Jessica looked up at her sister and offered her a smile that to Hayes looked more like she was baring her teeth in warning.

"I told Mom I would talk to Hayes about not helping him with inventory Sunday. I can probably do brunch."

Amelia peeked at Hayes.

"I suppose I can do it without you." He didn't try to add

anything to his tone, anything to make him sound grouchy or irritated. He had been told on more than one occasion that grouchy and irritated was his usual demeanor.

Jessica didn't look at him, but he saw her eyebrows jump slightly. Surprised by the life jacket he had thrown her, he guessed.

"Why do you hate Nolan?" Amelia asked her.

"I don't," Jessica said simply. Hayes had never known Jessica Bradshaw to *hate* anyone. But she did have a strong dislike for Nolan.

"Mom thinks you feel awkward because you can't get a date for Chelsea's wedding."

"Really?" Jessica looked at her sister with interest. Hayes polished off the pastry and wished for a bottle of Tums to chase it. This might get ugly; girl fights had stopped being interesting or sexy to him when he was eighteen.

"I mean, I know you don't like that I've been seeing Nolan, but Jess, I love him. I just want you to be happy for me."

"I am, Amelia." Jessica's voice was little more than a whisper.

"Really? You mean it?"

"I do."

"He's such a good guy. I mean, Jess, he said he would take you to the wedding."

Jessica stared at her sister like a deer caught in the headlights.

"He—? He what?"

"Yeah. I mean, if you guys get a room with two beds, right? He could go and be your date in public. And then you could just sleep in the same room. Chelsea knows him, but she wouldn't say anything to Rex's mom, would she? It's a win."

"What does Nolan get out of it?" Jessica asked with a frown. Amelia bit her lip, sending Hayes stomach south. He wanted to listen to girl talk even less than he wanted to watch a girl fight. But Jessica shook her head. "Never mind. I don't wanna know."

"So. He's prepared to, like, do the whole nine yards. He's got a nice tux. He could drive the Porsche—"

"Jess has a date for the wedding, Amelia," Hayes interrupted her. Both women turned to him with a look of surprise. But neither of them could be any more surprised by his words than he was. His heartbeat ramped up a bit under Amelia's suspicious gaze, in the crosshairs of Jessica's steely, frowning gaze.

"What?" Amelia asked. "You do?"

Jessica schooled her features into a calm, collected mask when her sister peeked at her.

"Yep." She sounded sincere, too. Even a bit bored.

"Who finally said yes?"

If he had any regrets about blurting it out that Jessica had a date, Amelia's last comment swallowed them whole.

"Me."

CHAPTER 7

*J*essica

Seven hours later, she still couldn't believe Hayes had volunteered himself to be her date for the wedding. She knew he had only done it because Amelia had shown up when she did. Because Amelia offered her boyfriend as a fake date. That was still wiggling around under her skin, irritating her as she watched Afton, their hostess, seat an older couple near the front windows. Who the hell did Nolan think he was? And what the hell was her sister's deal, acting like Nolan was swooping in to save the day?

But for Hayes to have just announced that he was going to the wedding with her? He had looked as shocked by his announcement as she and Amelia were. And just yesterday he had gone off on a tangent about how much he hated weddings and love and the big city. She appreciated that he had wanted to stand up for her when her little sister offered up her boyfriend, but there was no way in hell she was going to Chelsea and Rex's wedding with Hayes Kelley.

He had been exceptionally grouchy since she'd come in

earlier, which added to Jessica's belief that he had regretted the offer, the announcement, the second it popped out of his mouth. She hadn't had a chance to talk to him yet, to tell him thanks but no thanks. Amelia had plopped down on a stool at the island, apparently prepared to spend the day with Jessica. So Hayes had crushed the other pastry in the bag—the one he said he'd brought for her—and washed his hands and ducked out, leaving Jessica to bullshit her way through Amelia's questions.

Which she had done admirably, she thought. She had studied hotel and restaurant management for her hospitality degree in college, but the most valuable thing she had done in her four years was hone her bullshitting abilities. As far as she knew, Amelia one hundred percent believed Hayes was her plus one for Chelsea's wedding.

Which meant she had a lot of ground to cover and fast. Her sister wasn't a gossip; she wouldn't have run out and spread rumors that Jessica and Hayes were dating. But she would have told their parents by now. And since all of Holly Creek knew about the bet, it would soon be all over town. That would be one hell of a fire to put out. Jessica had been wracking her brain since Amelia left—since Hayes had declared himself her date, actually—trying to figure out who would go with her, so she and Hayes were both off the hook.

He would be impossible at a wedding. In fact, he would probably stand up when the officiant asked if anyone had a reason why Chelsea and Rex shouldn't get married. Jessica shuddered at the idea of Hayes rambling about weddings and love being bullshit and walking out. He'd probably have a damned flannel shirt on with his worn jeans. She would have to pry the stupid ballcap off his head.

Not to mention that she would have to listen to him for the drive. And it would be a drive, no train ride. No train from

Holly Creek to the city. Just another thing Rex's uppity groomsmen hated about Holly Creek. Hayes would insist on driving, and he would play Foo Fighters music all the way. And he would lecture Jessica on how dumb it was to spend money on a big wedding ceremony and a reception. That if a couple was that damned determined to be together, they ought to live together and invest the money saved on a wedding.

Nope.

Not happening.

She might throttle him before the weekend was over. Then she'd be up a creek—Holly Creek, because as much of a pain-in-the-ass as Hayes was, he was well-loved here—trying to sneak a black and blue, possibly dead Hayes back into town.

She would rather just lose the bet.

"Table seven needs attention."

Jessica jerked her gaze away from the front door. Jeez. How long had she been standing there staring? Thinking? She glanced at Matthias, one of the busboys, and then looked at table seven.

"There's no one at table seven."

"Right." The kid nodded. She liked Matthias; he was a good-looking, hard-working kid. Right now, she wondered if he needed glasses. "The table itself needs attention."

"Why?" She eyed the table, cataloging the rolled silverware bundled in burgundy linen napkins, the water glasses. The battery-operated candle was still lit. "What's wrong with it?" She finally looked back at Matthias. He hefted his tub of dishes and turned to walk backwards toward the kitchen.

"It's wobbling. Like it's got a short leg."

"What?" She shook her head. "But how did that happen? It was fine yesterday."

Matthias gave her a big shrug as he ducked into the kitchen. Jessica moved through the tables with ease, stopping at table seven. She drew her head back to look at it, at the legs, but they seemed fine. Feeling silly, she pressed her fingers gently on the corner of the table. And it wobbled. She groaned softly as she made her way back through the tables to the back of the restaurant. Still relatively early, it was quiet. Jessica smiled and spoke to the few patrons scattered across the dark, cozy room.

"What?" Hayes called as she stormed through the kitchen.

"Nothing."

"What?" he yelled again. She bumped the back doors of the kitchen and slipped out the hall to the back of the building. She needed a shim, but where would she find something like that? As far as she knew, they didn't have little slivers of wood laying around. Definitely none in her office. Hayes' office was hopeless, as decorated as an interrogation room. She hadn't been inside it lately, but as far as she knew, there was an empty desk in the center of the small room. No computer. No chair. No filing cabinet. Definitely nothing to wedge under the leg of table seven.

"Find anything?"

She looked over her shoulder when she heard Matthias' voice. The kid peeked his head out the door and watched her. He should be in the movies with his dark skin and dark hair close-cropped, always neat, never out of place. If he were ten years older, Jessica would ask him to go with her to the wedding. She wasn't sure he was even nineteen yet. Even the thought of dancing or walking arm-in-arm with him made her feel like a creepy old cougar.

"No." She shook her head. "I have not found anything."

"What about a matchbook?"

"Worth a shot, but I'm fresh out. You got any?" She headed back to the door and thanked him when he pushed it open wider and held it for her.

"No, but Hayes does."

"What?" She looked over her shoulder at him. Hayes had a pack of cigarettes on the corner of his desk. It had been sitting there long enough that it was dusty. For all she knew, the cigarettes might crumble if he tapped one out too hard. He took one out back every night after close and held it while he rode out the evening's adrenaline rush. And then put it back and walked away.

She had never seen a lighter or a book of matches around the place.

"Under the bar."

"Where?"

"I'll show you." Matthias nodded for her to follow him. They marched back through the kitchen. Hayes was busy with a skillet of mushroom risotto, but he must have looked up as she and Matthias reached the front door, because he hollered at her again.

"What?"

"Table issue," she called in response. "I'm on it."

Matthias led her to the bar. Jessica noticed Afton seating a group of four. Table eleven.

"Did you tell Afton?" she asked Matthias.

"No." He squatted at the bar, pulled the small safe forward, and popped it open. There was nothing of value in it. A couple of notepads, a pack of gum, and apparently seven books of matches. Jessica took a couple from Matthias and turned them over and over in her hands. One was from the bar on Main Street. The other from a lounge in Atlantic City. As far as she knew, this safe had been here back before Hayes bought the place and turned it into Kelley's Chop House.

Now a little worry niggled at the back of her mind.

Was Hayes smoking? It wasn't her business, she decided as she headed to the dining area to table seven.

"Gimme a hand, Afton."

The girl joined her at the table.

"Got a wobbly leg," Jessica mumbled, still wondering if Hayes was sneaking cigarettes. Telling herself it wasn't her business. Arguing with herself that it was her business, because even if he was a grouch, he was her boss. And she liked him.

Afton tilted the table as Jessica squatted and slipped the matchbooks under it.

"Try it." She looked up at the girl, who set the table down and then leaned a bit on the corner. Still wobbly, but somewhat better. At least they wouldn't have a weekend crowd. "Don't seat anyone here unless you have to. I'll make a note to find a shim tomorrow before we open."

"Got it." Afton nodded. "Nancy Higgins called. She wants to talk to you about booking the room upstairs for her office Christmas party."

"Seriously?" Jessica snorted. "She's a little late, isn't she?"

"I told her that. She wants you to call her."

"Joy." Jessica nodded. "Will do."

Jessica glanced at the bar as she headed to her office. Matthias had put the little safe back, but she still wondered if Hayes was smoking and if he was, why did she feel so betrayed?

CHAPTER 8

*H*ayes

"Five minutes table ten," Matthias called as he cleared the kitchen doors and set his tub of dishes on the stainless-steel counter. Hayes glanced at the kid as he started rinsing the glasses and loading them in the dishwasher.

"How's that gnocchi coming?" he hollered over his shoulder.

"Plating it."

Hayes nodded and turned his attention back to the salmon portion he had just plated. He grabbed the lemon herbed couscous and arranged it on the plate just as Capri burst through the doors to pick up the order.

"Matthias," she glanced at the kid, "got a spill on five."

"Broken glass?" Hayes asked.

"Nope. Just a white wine spill." She picked up the salmon dish and the pork medallion dish and headed back to the dining area.

"Gnocchi," Kyler Tremont, Hayes' sous chef, said as he reached around Hayes to put the dish down.

"Last order in, right?" Hayes glanced at Kyler who confirmed with a quick nod. He lifted his arm and wiped the side of his face on his t-shirt sleeve. The kitchen felt like the tenth circle of hell at the moment. He couldn't wait to start the cleanup and get outside.

Jessica had been busy tonight. Seemed like every time he had looked away from his food prep or the stovetop, she was rushing in one set of kitchen doors and out the other. He had asked a few times what was going on, but she hadn't stopped to talk. Their choppy, nonexistent conversation felt like a game of Marco Polo that neither of them was bound to win.

He wondered if she was upset about earlier. God knows, he was. How in the hell those words had come out of his mouth, he had no idea. Sure, it had bugged him to see that look of indignation on her face, the way Amelia's—*Nolan's*—offer had taken her by surprise. But why hadn't he just said something else? Like *Jessica doesn't need your charity* or *your leftovers*. Both sounded harsh, and though he didn't mean to attack Amelia, Jessica *didn't* need either. He could have shown his support for Jessica in another way.

As it was, he now had a late December date in the big city with his restaurant manager. And if he told her he had changed his mind, she would be right back to scrambling to figure something else out.

Later, the bar still open, but the kitchen closed and spotless for the night, Hayes strolled into the front of the restaurant and moseyed up to the bar. Afton had clocked out and gone home; Matthias and the other busboy had gone home. Only Hampton and Jessica remained out front.

"Whatchu need, boss?" Hampton flashed him a smile. A diamond stud glittered from Hampton's right nostril. The left side of his neck was covered in tattoos, so much so that Hayes had known the guy for fifteen years and had no idea what they were. Still, Hampton wore his hair in a military cut, and he dressed in a black button-down shirt with neat jeans every shift. He was good with the drinks and even better with their customers.

"Gimme a pour of Blanton's," he answered, eyes on Jessica at the opposite end of the bar talking to one of their regular couples. He was aware of Hampton pouring the Blanton's as he watched Jessica waving her hands frantically and laughing while she talked.

He wondered what she was saying. Half the time, she rattled so much and so fast, Hayes didn't have a clue. What would five minutes in her brain be like? After watching her a moment longer, he decided he didn't want to know.

"Busy night," Hampton told him as he slid the Glencairn to him over the bar. "I think the holidays have officially started."

"Wonderful."

If there was anything Hayes hated more than weddings, it was the Christmas holidays. People, ex-girlfriends in particular, always wanted to pick his brain, figure out why he hated things that made most people happy. He didn't—not *all* things that made people happy. Like dogs, for instance. He liked dogs.

"I'm gonna go cool off." He flicked his gaze to Hampton. "Holler if you need something."

"I gotchu boss." The man nodded as Hayes turned and moved back through the hall and the kitchen to the back door. It was cold tonight, but even with that harsh December chill in the air, it would take a bit to cool him off. He loved being in the kitchen. He loved food. Loved making food that people raved about. And if the holiday season brought more people out and about and ultimately to his restaurant for fine dining, he would deal with Christmas.

At least he and his dad didn't do the whole bullshit gift

exchange thing. They'd done it before his mom passed away. She used to fix big dinners, and Hayes' aunts and uncles, cousins—hell, sometimes even neighbors—would join them. They gorged themselves on his mom's turkey and stuffing and then turned around and stuffed themselves on her pies, and then later while playing games, they pretended they were hungry, that they hadn't just eaten enough to feed a small country, and they ate his mom's homemade cookies and candies.

They had always had a gift exchange. No matter who came to dinner, he or she didn't show up empty-handed. Simple gifts. Always wrapped in pretty paper and bows. They'd play games and pass the variety of boxes around and around until finally the timer went off, and everyone kept whatever was in their hands. His parents had given him gifts through the years; even Santa had stopped at his house when he was a kid—proof to him even then that Santa was bullshit, because Hayes should have been on the naughty list every year.

A lot had changed after his mom died. He still visited his dad; in fact, he was usually at the house every day for one thing or another. They watched football and hockey together over beers and pizza, and even on the holidays, Hayes made sure to be around for his dad. But the house was quiet and dark. His dad had thrown the old artificial tree out the year after Mom was gone. The old man never took the box of Christmas decorations or vinyl records out anymore.

Hayes supposed there was still some level of comfort. Both he and his dad had roofs over their heads and food to live on. But there was no light, little joy, left in their lives.

He flinched at the sound of the back door banging open. Assuming there was trouble up front, Hayes jumped quickly to his feet and turned, only to find Jessica glowering at him.

"What's wrong?"

She tugged on her wool coat as she stepped outside and let the door close behind her.

"Are you smoking?" she asked.

"What?" He looked around, genuinely confused by her out-of-the-blue accusation. "No."

"Don't bullshit me, Hayes Kelley."

He held his hands up—the Glencairn in one and the same unlit cigarette from the other night in his other hand. Instead of reassuring her, his gesture apparently enraged Jessica. She stomped toward him and snatched the cigarette from his hand.

"What're—?" He cringed when she broke it in two and carried it out to the dumpster in the alley. When she turned and walked back to him, Hayes nodded and sat back down. "Thanks. Those suckers aren't cheap."

"So quit buying them."

"What bug crawled up your ass today, Bradshaw?"

"I wanna know," she stopped in front of him, "why in the hell there are a bunch of match books under the bar."

"I have no idea." He shrugged and sipped his bourbon.

"It'll kill you, Hayes. First your mom—"

Not in need of the reminder, Hayes stared at her silently and held up a hand to stop her.

"I'm well aware that my mom died of lung cancer and that my dad has emphysema. Thank you, though, for the public—"

"Don't be such a smartass!" She leaned forward and smacked his shoulder. "Quit smok—"

"I quit years ago!" he yelled as he dodged another swing. "I have no idea why the matches are there. Maybe Doug and Linda Pomeroy kept them there when they owned the place."

"You didn't do, like, a thorough cleaning?" she asked, considerably quieter now.

"No. I didn't. We never closed. Never remodeled. You know that, Bradshaw. You've been around all this time, too."

She harrumphed and sat down beside him on the table.

"I just..." She shook her head. "Somebody's gotta take care of you, and I guess as your work wife, that's me. I don't wanna see you smoking."

"Work wife?" he repeated with a cough. Sure, it was a fair enough label for who she was to him at the Chop House. But on the heels of his damned mouth announcing to Amelia earlier that he was taking Jessica to the wedding, it made his throat ache. Like his tie was too tight. The tie he wasn't wearing.

"Right-hand woman," she mumbled, eyes on the dumpster as if she worried the cigarette would climb out of it and come back to him.

"I'm not smoking," he repeated. "Why in the hell are we even talking about this? What made you go digging around under the bar for match books?"

"Mmm." She nodded and looked back at him. "Table seven has a wobbly leg. Couldn't find a shim."

"So, you stacked a couple of books of matches under it." He frowned. "Classy, Bradshaw."

"The only person seated there tonight was Ellen Vedenhaup. I'm sure she didn't notice a thing."

Despite himself, Hayes had to laugh. Ellen Vedenhaup was one of the town drunks. Sweet, little old lady, always dressed to the nines. Walked everywhere she went. Enjoyed her whiskies just a little too much.

"Nice."

They exchanged a small smile.

"What're you drinking?" she asked him.

He handed it to her as he spoke, "Blanton's."

She took a small sip and closed her eyes as she swallowed. The look of satisfaction on her face startled him. Pure, smug, pleasure. He wouldn't have been surprised if she had moaned out loud. She looked blissful, like—

Hayes gave himself a firm mental shake.

Do not go there.

"Hayes, I think Amelia's really in love with Nolan."

Hayes took a deep breath and snatched his glass back from her.

"I think she should dump him."

"I do, too. I'm worried about her."

Worrying wasn't his bag, either. Female emotions all boggled his brain. He didn't know what to say to make any woman feel better. Ever. Definitely not right now, in this moment. And he didn't want to take the time to figure it out.

Before he could say anything, even some bullshit thing to change the subject, Jessica turned and hit him with those bright green eyes again.

"I'm not taking you to the wedding."

CHAPTER 9

*J*essica

Hayes breathed in so deeply, his nostrils flared. She couldn't miss the slump of his shoulders, either. He was relieved. Jessica got it; he had thrown her a rope so she could save face in front of her little sister. And he had probably been spinning his wheels since he left her house earlier today, wondering how the hell to get out of it.

"Good." He nodded. Took another swallow of the bourbon. Jessica reached toward him and took the glass, wishing for something higher proof, even as she took a healthy-sized drink. Hayes frowned when he took the glass back. "Damn. There's a whole bar just inside."

"You know what I wish?"

"That this glass was full again?" He quirked an eyebrow at her and flinched at the hard look she gave him. "Maybe I was projecting my wishes onto you, there."

"I wish Chelsea and Rex would run away and get married in Paris or something."

"Ever been?" His voice was gruff.

"No, but that's not the point."

"The point," he flicked his gaze to hers and looked away, "is that you don't want to go to the wedding. You don't want to deal with your date. You don't want to be in the city. You don't want to have to mingle with Rex's groomsmen. Amiright?"

"Smartass."

"So, who'd you find?"

"What?"

"If I'm off the hook, who did you find? Someone come in tonight?"

"No." She shook her head.

"Stirling change his mind? I thought he was going to see his—"

"No, Hayes. I'm not taking a date."

"This again." He sighed and drained the bourbon in his glass.

"You just said *off the hook*. Like, you're relieved I'm not gonna hold you to some bullshit announcement you made to my sister."

"Well, you tricked me."

Jessica laughed softly. "I appreciate the gesture, but I'll be fine. And if you were worried that I would take Nolan up on his offer—"

"Nope."

"Good."

"What kinda wedding do you want?" he asked after a few moments of silence.

"What?"

"When you do it. When you get that big ass ball and chain attached, how're you gonna do it? Big wedding?"

"So romantic," she mumbled.

"Lisa wanted the whole nine yards."

"Lisa," she repeated.

"Oh, come on. Everyone knows about Lisa leaving Hayes at the altar. It's a folk story here in Holly Creek."

Jessica watched him for a moment. Shoulders raised and chest puffed up like he was a big shot, totally over the heartbreak. Above the drama.

"I didn't know her name was Lisa."

"Lisa Dugan. Blond bombshell."

"Why did she leave?"

Hayes twisted his lips a bit, as if he was thinking about how to answer her. Finally, he shrugged and glanced at her.

"Grass is always greener, right?"

"She cheated?"

"No." He sighed and shook his head. "No. I just wasn't enough for her. Fast enough. Ambitious enough."

"You work your ass off here," Jessica reminded him.

"Right?" He nodded. "It's a successful business, if I do say so myself."

"It is," she agreed.

"Holly Creek is too small. She hated small town life. She hated everyone knowing her business. She hated that I worked too much. I didn't own it at the time. But we had talked about it. I told her I was saving. That I wanted to buy it from Doug."

"And that wasn't enough?"

"At first, she was pretty into it. But no. Eventually, she hated the place. She hated everything about Holly Creek. She hated Christmas, which ironically, was kind of the one thing I could understand."

Jessica huddled deeper into her coat, still shivering a little. She dragged her eyes away from Hayes, not wanting him to feel exposed after revealing that little bit of himself. She wasn't the type to gawk at mangled cars after a traffic accident, either.

"I don't want a big wedding," she said after a few moments.

"No?"

"No." She shook her head.

"Justice of the peace?"

"Maybe something bigger than that." She shot him a smile. "No *big* dress. No slew of bridesmaids. I don't want a big reception."

"Why not?"

"Why waste the money?" She shrugged. "I'd rather have a simple wedding and a great honeymoon."

"You can have a great honeymoon without money."

Jessica chuckled. "True. But I meant location, not a way to pass the time."

"If you're on a honeymoon, what difference does it make if you're in a hotel somewhere in Indiana or in a cabana on la Playa del Carmen?"

"I'm beginning to see what Lisa meant about you."

Hayes leaned forward to rest his elbows on his knees. His shoulders shook with his laughter.

"Look, I don't want to. I really don't," he admitted. "Because in my mind, Chelsea and Rex will be divorced before they celebrate five years together."

"No. They won't." She shook her head.

"Let's bet on it."

"I'm losing my ass in the current bet, thank you very much," she reminded him.

"I'll go. With you. Unless you find a date."

"Why would you do that?" She tipped her head and studied his face. The look of sincerity was gone instantly, but she had seen it. The idea of a high society anything pained Hayes Kelley, but he seemed sincere about helping her out.

"Told ya." He stood up. "I don't wanna see any video of you doing the chicken dance. And if you donate money to a women's foundation or something—"

"What's wrong with a women's foundation?" she argued.

"Nothing, but why not donate to something for kids?"

"What?" In a rush, she climbed off the table to follow him to the building. "What? Kids?"

"Yeah, you know. Short people. Goofy vocabularies. They drool and shit."

"I know what kids are. I'm just surprised you do," she answered as she trailed him inside.

"I'm not dancing," he called as he banged the men's room door open. "I'll wear a damned monkey suit. But I draw the line at dancing."

Jessica stared at the door as it swung shut.

Hayes Kelley in a tuxedo. Damned if she wasn't curious now.

CHAPTER 10

*H*ayes
      His dad was muttering something unkind about someone, but with his head under the kitchen sink, Hayes couldn't hear him. He didn't particularly care. When his dad stopped talking, Hayes would mumble something in response. His dad didn't hear well anymore, so he wouldn't know what Hayes said. It was a fun game. They played it all the time.

The kitchen sink was leaking. His dad was sure the back burner on the stove wasn't working. Hayes had considered reminding his dad he didn't cook, so it really didn't matter if the stove worked or not. But on occasion Hayes cooked something for them over here, and now and then, his dad did fix oatmeal for himself.

So, here he was. Playing handyman before heading off to slave at the Chop House later. Not that he minded. Hell, he didn't have anything to do at home today. He was good on groceries. Might as well tinker at his dad's house before his dad got tired of waiting on him and tried to tackle the problem himself.

And then he would grab a quick shower at home and get to the restaurant.

He and Jessica had sparred every night this week. Out back. After close. In the cold. There hadn't been anymore talk about the wedding. That was a relief. If he had to go with her to the city, he didn't want to have to talk it to death. Instead, they'd debated cryptocurrencies replacing cash and dogs versus cats— interesting, as Hayes knew on every other occasion animals had come up, Jessica had been a dog person, but the other night, she was all in for cats. He was pretty sure she had argued just to argue. They talked about clowns in horror movies, but they both agreed clowns were creepy, so there hadn't been much to debate there.

When he finally climbed out from under the cabinet and flipped to kneel in front of it, his dad had stopped talking. Hayes, hands now wrapped around the porcelain sink over his head, leaning in to study the pipes, looked over his shoulder to where his dad sat at the dinette table where Hayes had eaten meals with his parents.

"Dad."

Nose in a book, he either ignored him or didn't hear him. Hayes assumed it was the first. Wilson Kelley was an avid reader. The man knew shit about things Hayes had never even heard of. Quantum-physics—sure; Hayes was familiar with the word. Extending the life of quantum coherence? Not a fucking clue.

Hayes was educated; he might have been a hell-raiser when he was younger, but he had graduated. From college, too, with a degree in business. He hadn't gone to culinary school; he had learned to cook by watching his mom. Helping his mom. When he was a teenager, he got interested in cooking shows. When he started as a busboy at what was now the Chop House, he already wanted to work in the kitchen, already had thoughts of buying the place. But no, he didn't have a bunch of useless, random factoids in his head. Like his dad.

"Dad," he said again, louder this time.

"Hmm?" The man looked up, his hand spread out to hold his page in his book.

"Turn the faucet on for me," he told him.

"Lemme finish this chapter." Wilson ducked his head again.

"Unreal," Hayes grumbled. Two seconds later, his dad stood and closed his book. He crossed the room and flipped the faucet on.

"How's it look?"

Head back inside the cabinet, Hayes studied the pipes. "I think it's good."

"Good." His dad nodded as Hayes slowly straightened and stood at the sink. "Your phone's been buzzing over there."

"Not my phone." Hayes shook his head. "I don't use it for that."

"What do you use it for?"

"Calendar." He shrugged. "To tell time."

"Well, it buzzed," his dad said again. "Someone named Bradshaw."

"You looked at my phone?" Hayes yelped. Maybe he was pretending to be a little indignant about that so he could ignore the little zap of tingly, weird energy in his gut. What the hell was Jessica calling him about?

"Guy said he needs to get a gift and wants your input."

"You read my texts?" Hayes groaned.

Every contact in his phone was listed by last name. His dad had met Jessica on numerous occasions, but he probably had never been introduced to her by her full name.

And what the hell? Why would Jessica want his input on a gift? Hayes hadn't bought anyone a gift since he splurged on the diamond ring for Lisa. The one she had tried to give back to him. Dumbass that he was, he had refused it. What the hell would he want with an engagement ring he bought for a woman who didn't want it? Well, he'd done some growing up in the years since then, and he had wished a hundred times over that he had taken the ring back. Hell, he could have sold it and made some kind of money back on it.

"You Christmas shopping?" his dad asked him, bringing him back to the present.

"No."

"You hanging out with guys now?"

Hayes had been staring at the stove, wondering if he really wanted to get into it today. Now he jerked his gaze to his dad's. When he was younger, Hayes had always hung out with a group of friends. Mostly guys, sure. While he wasn't the high school quarterback, he'd had a group of friends he had fun with.

At the moment, it felt like his dad was suggesting something else. Something else entirely.

"Bradshaw, Dad." He scratched a spot over his eye and turned to the table. No, he did not want to look at the stove today. It wasn't like it would be a lot of work. Probably the burner needed replaced. Wasn't a place here in Holly Creek to get another one; he would have to go to Cooperstown and even then, it would probably have to be ordered.

His dad stepped out of his way as Hayes leaned over the table and snatched his phone up. He tapped the screen, opened his text messages—a list of three threads—and opened the message from Jessica. Just as his dad had said, she did indeed want his opinion on something. He stifled a groan and turned his phone to his dad.

"Bradshaw. It's a last name."

"Mmm." His dad nodded. "Who is it?"

"Jessica."

"Ah." His dad grinned this time. "Your work wife."

"My restaurant manager," he corrected him, bristling at that word again.

"Pick me up some Chinese food while you're out, will ya?"

His dad would eat whatever Hayes fixed him, but he also liked fast food. Unhealthy snack foods. Ice cream. Hell, Hayes couldn't even blame him for that because he liked all of the above, too.

"Sure, Dad. I'll do that. I'm gonna meet Jessica. I'll get to your stove tomorrow."

"Yeah." His dad picked up the book from the table. He had taken the dust cover off the hardback; he had done that since Hayes was a kid. But Hayes caught some of the gold lettering on the spine. Enough to know his dad was reading something about the Industrial Revolution.

He watched his dad move through the kitchen and open dining space to the living room. He sat down in his recliner, put the footrest up, and opened his book. Hayes felt a pang of sadness for him. Love had worked for his parents; it was supposed to last forever. But it didn't. And in a committed, loving relationship, someone would always lose. Just another reason Hayes had no interest.

"General Tso's chicken," his dad called. "And lo mein. Two fortune cookies."

Grateful for the slap of reality to pull him from his maudlin thoughts, Hayes laughed to himself.

"Got it."

CHAPTER 11

Jessica

As much as she loved Holly Creek, Jessica had to admit she wasn't going to find a fitting wedding gift for Chelsea here. Oh sure, there were things Chelsea loved at the craft store. Cute little kitschy decorations and craft supplies she would have loved back in the day. But nothing that said wedding gift, most definitely nothing that said *high society, my mother-in-law is a snob*, wedding gift.

She shouldn't be that way. Jessica was a peacemaker. Always had been. Probably one of the big reasons why she had so much trouble trying to tell her sister that she thought her boyfriend was a tool and why it irked her that even her parents were fooled. Miriam Buchanan, Rex's mother, wasn't Jessica's favorite person, but she didn't have to be. If Chelsea got along with her, good for her. That was all that mattered.

"What?" The deadpan voice was familiar. Not comforting. Nope. *Familiar.* Jessica looked over her shoulder as Hayes stepped up behind her. She sipped from her coffee and took him in. Jeans. Brown Carhartt coat unzipped over a black t-shirt. The corner of a black and gray flannel shirt stuck out at the waist band of his coat. The hat of the day faded black—backwards, but Jessica knew without seeing it that it said *Ford* on it.

She'd sent him an SOS about shopping. For the hell of it. Not because she thought he would show up and offer opinions. Hayes loved food—eating it, cooking it, looking at it—but even grocery shopping pained him. Wasn't anything physical. He just hated crowded aisles and bumping into people.

Which one tended to do often in Holly Creek.

"I don't know what to get Chels for the wedding."

To her surprise, Hayes pointed at the shop window in front of her. She had been looking at an old-fashioned sewing machine. Not with any intention of purchasing it. Just wasting time before she went home to get ready for work.

"Get that."

She burst into laughter. "I am sure Chelsea and Rex want that hideous thing in their apartment."

"Give them cash," he suggested.

Without deciding to, they started walking side by side down Main Street.

"Too impersonal," she argued.

"Cookware."

"Says the chef."

"Whaddaya want from me?" he asked with a dramatic shrug. "Three suggestions, all shot down."

She ignored his complaint. "I need to go to Cooperstown."

"Order something online."

"Maybe a crystal dish," she continued to think out loud.

"Good idea." He nodded. Jessica glanced at him, shocked by his words. "Everyone needs a good crystal dish in their house."

"You're such a guy." She rolled her eyes.

"I am," he agreed. "Cash is the most useful gift. They can do with it whatever they want."

"First of all," she looked up at him as they walked, "they have cash. So. Much. Cash. Remember? Rex Buchanan?"

Hayes stared at her, deadpan, clearly not impressed.

"And I don't. What's a hundred dollar check from me gonna mean to them?"

"A five-dollar bill from you should mean the world to them," he answered. "Because it's the thought, Jess. It's that you live here in Holly Creek, and like the rest of us mere mortals here, you don't sleep in satin sheets, and you don't drink champagne for breakfast. You don't have a Mercedes. If you give them five bucks, a hundred bucks, whatever? You're giving them what you can afford. Chelsea's your friend. She knows who you are. She knows who all of you girls are."

"How do you know?" she asked him.

"Know what?" He frowned and reached for her coffee. She watched uncertainly as he took a big drink.

"That I don't sleep in satin sheets."

He nearly spit the coffee out, but Jessica wasn't sure if that was because of what she had said or because she was drinking a mocha.

"I made an assumption," he grumbled and handed her the cup back.

"What? Because I'm boring? Because I don't live in the city? Or because I sleep in fleece llama pajamas?"

She had to hold down her excitement when he cracked a grin.

"What the hell are you drinking?"

"Café mocha."

"Why?"

"Because it's Christmas, and I wanted to do something fun."

"It's not Christmas. It's the first week of December."

"We live in Holly Creek, Hayes," she reminded him. "It's been Christmas for a month now."

"How old were you when you stopped believing in Santa Claus?"

"Who says I stopped believing?" She tipped her head back and looked at him with narrowed eyes. He opened his mouth to say something, caught himself, and simply laughed and shook his head.

"I need to get my dad something to eat."

"You don't cook for him?"

"I was at his house when you texted. He asked for Chinese food."

"Why don't we have a Chinese restaurant here?"

"Too small," he answered. "The Chinese stuff at the grocery store's not bad."

Jessica stared at him wide-eyed. "Wow. Is that a confession? Do you actually eat that stuff?"

He shrugged. "Maybe."

"Do you exchange gifts?" she asked him. "You and your dad?"

"No. I fix a pot of chili on Christmas Day. We eat it. Drink beer. And watch football."

"You don't even watch Christmas movies?"

"Why would we?"

"We do."

"Color me surprised." He arched his eyebrows.

"I need to go Christmas shopping, too." She sighed. "I guess I can see if I can peel Amelia away from Nolan for a day."

"I'll go with you."

Jessica froze in her tracks and shot him a frown. "Who *are* you? And what have you done with Hayes Kelley? The grouch? You know him? Hates people. Holidays. Laughter. Life."

"Haha." He rolled his eyes, but she could see a smile playing at his lips. "I'm probably going to have to go to Cooperstown anyway. One of Dad's burners isn't working. I'm assuming I'll need to go there to even order one."

"Two birds with one stone."

"Something like that." He nodded.

"It's a date."

"It's not." He cringed. "It's not a date."

"Just so you know," she tipped her head, "in case we end up having another date between now and the wedding? I don't put out. On the third date."

"Jesus," he muttered and squeezed his eyes closed.

"Not to mention, this guy I know told me I don't have to pay for dates with sexual favors."

"Nope." He shook his head. "Nope. Nope. Don't say that to me. Don't say those words to me."

"You don't do sex?" she teased.

"Not with little girls, no."

"Little girls," she repeated. "Right. Okay."

"You were eleven when I was eighteen."

"Mm-hmm," she agreed. "That establishes that I'm younger than you, Old Man. But not that I'm a little girl."

They crossed a street and slowed to a stop in front of the grocery store. Jessica tipped her head and studied him with a frown.

"What?" He sighed, as if he was exhausted, maybe tired of her.

Jessica laughed softly. "Just wondering if that's why you're always so cranky." She shrugged and backed away from him with a grin. "See ya later, Old Man."

CHAPTER 12

*H*ayes

"What the hell is this?" He tied the apron around his waist, chin tilted down, but his eyes roamed the kitchen, looking for Jessica.

"What's what?" she hollered from somewhere behind him.

Hayes spun around as he straightened. The music playing was pleasant enough, soft and easy to listen to. It was the lyrics he had an issue with. He narrowed his eyes at Jessica as she approached him. Dressed in slacks a shade just off white and a deep green blouse, she looked ready for the holidays. She had piled her hair up in some kind of messy knot at the back of her head. Unless she had won the lottery in the last few hours, he assumed the clip in her hair was covered in rhinestones and not diamonds. Didn't matter. Her eyes outshined the rhinestones—those on the clip and the fine, sparkling strands that dangled from her ears.

Remembering that he wanted to pummel her for the song choice and not stand here and drool over her, Hayes gave himself a mental shake and stepped toward the stainless-steel counter. He needed the space.

"The song."

"It's a Christmas song, Hayes." She folded her arms over her chest, enjoying his obvious discomfort. What she didn't know was that he was far more flustered by her blouse, the silk clinging to her breasts now emphasized by the fold of her arms than he was the song wishing for snow.

"Tempting fate," he muttered, ignoring the fact that his words could apply to the way she was dressed and the way she stood in front of him. Again, he was referring to the song.

"Christmas comes every year. Whether we want it to or not," she reminded him.

Hayes wondered if there had ever been a year when she didn't want Christmas to come.

"I meant the snow. Wishing for snow."

Jessica snorted softly and shrugged. "We live in upstate New York. And it's December. Embrace it, Hayes. Enjoy the season."

"It's not the season yet," he called after her as she made her way on through the kitchen. She walked steady on the high black heels, no faltering, no wobbling. When she waitressed for him, she wore the simple black pants and tops the rest of the Chop House waiters wore. Hayes wouldn't admit to anyone that even then he had thought she was pretty. She had worn black loafers or tennis shoes back then.

Okay, so if he was being honest, and if he couldn't be honest with himself he had a problem, he much preferred Jessica in the dressy, professional clothing she wore now. The colors brought out her eyes and the flush in her cheeks. Hayes knew sometimes the pink in her cheeks was due to working hard, rushing around, and getting warm. But he also knew she loved what she was doing; Jessica loved working with his staff, and she loved talking to people out front.

At the swinging door, she turned to him and tipped her head again. Her slight hesitation amused him. A low laugh rumbled up inside him. Surprised at himself, he rested his hands on his hips.

"You're thinking about flipping me off right now, aren't you?"

Her laughter pinged somewhere in his gut and spread something warm and almost cheerful through him. Damn. Jessica Bradshaw was kind of like whiskey.

"Cheers, Kelley."

He didn't even flinch when she called him by his surname. Often, people who didn't know him well assumed his given name was Kelley and his surname was Hayes. And sometimes people he had known forever, people who should know better, mixed his names up. It drove Hayes crazy. Which unfortunately, Jessica knew. She liked to pull that one out now and then and use it on him.

Oddly enough, it really never bothered him when she did it. Mostly because he knew she was teasing him. This time, though, it made him laugh. He watched her slip through the doors and made himself turn his attention back to the kitchen.

It was steady busy all night. Again. It would only get crazier from here until after December. Even though he argued with Jessica that it wasn't the holiday season, he knew the people of Holly Creek were well into their Christmas season, the celebrating and the shopping. Which was good for him. He didn't have anyone to shop for, he and his dad didn't care to do much in the way of holiday shopping, so he would keep his restaurant open for weary shoppers and travelers and make bank while he was at it.

Hampton and Jessica were both occupied when he slipped up front to survey the dining area and bar after he closed the kitchen down. Hampton was deep in conversation with three gentlemen at the bar as he mixed what appeared to be Old Fashioneds for them. Jessica stood at a table across the dining room, talking animatedly with the two couples seated there. Even after the crazy running around, helping servers, offering a hand at the bar, and talking to their customers all evening, she looked fresh and—

Happy.

Not exactly where he had been going with that thought, but his brain woke up and cut any other thought off. Just because he was stuck being Jessica's date for Chelsea Calhoun's wedding didn't mean he had to go thinking weird thoughts about her.

Kind of odd, though, that he was. Because after Lisa, other than the few one-night flings that had been unsatisfying and a little off-putting, Hayes hadn't cared to look at any women, let alone think those kinds of thoughts.

Jessica moved, shifted a bit on her feet. As if she could feel him watching her in her periphery vision, she turned and met his eyes across the room. Hayes was suddenly aware of the music playing; still Christmas, but this time it was a jazzy sounding instrumental version of "Have Yourself a Merry Little Christmas." Jessica's smile aimed directly at him made his feet sweat.

What the fuck?

He offered her a tiny nod and turned away. His eyes dragged over the remaining customers—still three tables occupied. He watched them all for a moment. At each table, there were smiles and friendly faces. People talking. Listening. Laughing.

This is what he had wanted when he bought the restaurant and turned it into the Chop House. Sure, he loved food. *Cooking* food. *Looking at it. Eating it.* But he loved cooking food for others. He loved that these families, these friends, were gathered at his place, eating food he had prepared for them, while they enjoyed each other's company.

Finally, he shifted his gaze to the Christmas tree Jessica and Capri had decorated. It looked good. He wasn't one to stand around and get sentimental about trees or decorations like snow-covered ceramic village pieces. But he knew class when he saw it. Jessica Bradshaw brought class and atmosphere to the Chop House. She was indispensable. He needed to remember that.

With Hampton still busy with the gentlemen at the bar, Hayes grabbed a bottle of Elijah Craig and poured a bit in a Glencairn. He topped the bottle, nodded at the gentlemen with Hampton when they glanced his way, and then slipped back through the kitchen to go to his office. Just a pit stop to grab a new cigarette. Jessica wouldn't scare him off that habit, that ritual.

He flipped his office light on and stepped inside to pull the top desk drawer open. Something was off. The lighting was different. Hayes dropped his head back to look up at the plain fixture on the ceiling. Same as always—simple fixture, all the bulbs were lit. Stumped, he looked around and finally noticed the tiny Christmas tree in the corner. Couldn't have been more than two feet tall, set upon a small table. The white lights had added an odd glow to the room. Forgetting the cigarettes for now, Hayes jammed his hands in his pockets and stepped closer to the tree. To investigate. Not admire. Tiny red and green ornaments hung from the branches. Rather than an angel at the top of the tree, there was a stuffed troll dressed in red, green, and white tied to the top.

Bradshaw.

He laughed despite himself. Pulled his right hand from his pocket and flicked the nose on the troll, wondering if it was all she could find in her search for a Scrooge decoration or if she was calling him a troll. The grin still on his face, he turned back to his desk, snatched the pack of cigarettes, and tapped one out. He curled his fingers around it, put the pack back on his desk, and looked at the tree again. It was okay. The hell of it was, he wasn't in his office much at all, so he wasn't going to see it much.

Outside, he shivered a bit as he climbed up to sit on the picnic table. He had pulled his flannel shirt on over the t-shirt he had worked in, but he wasn't sure it would be enough for long out here. He sipped the bourbon as he rubbed his thumb down the length of the cigarette as he waited for Jessica to join him.

CHAPTER 13

*J*essica

Jessica flagged Amelia down when she saw her step inside Brewed Awakening. Her sister acknowledged her with a smile and a nod before grabbing her place in line. Jessica picked up her mocha as she turned her attention back to her phone. Specifically, the picture of the Christmas tree she had put up in Hayes' office the other day.

She had done it on a whim. Just to mess with him. Jessica had been needling him with Christmas music in early December (sometimes late November and once on Halloween Night a few years ago) for years. He didn't disappoint. Hayes never got angry—not with her, anyway. And if he did, it would be over something more important than Christmas music, something dealing with the business, whether it be a mistake on a purchase invoice or an altercation with a customer.

But Jessica knew she was safe to mess with him about Christmas stuff. Speaking of which—

She tapped out a quick text to him.

Kelley's Table. Kelley's Family Table.

Before she even put her phone down, it pinged with his response.

No.

Jessica could just see his face. Set in stone. No frown, but no smile. Just there, empty of amusement or emotion.

Kelley's Christmas Table.

Again his answer was immediate.

NO.

Ooh. All caps. He meant business on that one.

At Brewed Awakening. Want me to bring you anything?

No.

She was still snickering when her sister joined her at the round two-top table near the window. It was colder sitting by a window, but Jessica was dressed for the weather. Jeans, sweater, and boots. As much as she didn't care for crowds, she was a people watcher. Besides, Holly Creek was dressed for the holidays; Jessica couldn't take her eyes off Main Street. Moving north with her family when she was fourteen had been hard on her. Leaving her friends and the house she had grown up in, moving away from her school and her favorite teachers, moving somewhere north where winters would be much colder than they were in the Midwest—she shuddered now at the memory.

The only thing that had consoled her that first year here was the over-the-top ridiculous Christmas spirit in the small town. Her family had moved into the bungalow where her parents still lived now in June, and Holly Creek had rolled out the holly and ivy and elves and Santa and *everything* Christmas she could have dreamt of to celebrate Christmas in July.

"What?" Amelia asked her now.

"Giving Hayes some shit." Jessica put her phone down and eyed Amelia's drink. "What're you having?"

"Sugar Cookie Latte. Wanna try it?"

"No, thanks." But she did log the information away so she could treat Hayes to one later.

"About that." Amelia folded her hands on the table and stared at Jessica boldly.

"What?"

"You and Hayes."

"What about me and Hayes?" Jessica asked with a frown.

"How long have you been seeing each other?"

"What?" If she had been taking a drink, she would be choking now.

"I guess Mom was right," Amelia mumbled more to herself than to Jessica. She took a drink and looked around. Jessica watched her, still amused and now a little annoyed because Amelia must really believe she and Hayes were dating.

And what about their mom? Being right?

"We're not seeing each other."

"Mmm." Amelia nodded.

"No." Jessica lifted her hand and snapped her fingers in front of Amelia's face. "Hello? Not seeing each other."

"Stop it." Amelia swatted her hand away. "I thought he was going with you to Chelsea's wedding."

"Yeah, as my plus one." Jessica shrugged and shook her head. "That doesn't mean we're dating."

"Oh." Amelia blinked. "Really?"

"Just friends," Jessica assured her.

"But you'll sleep with him, right? At the wedding?"

"Amelia—"

"At the *Plaza Hotel*? You'll be in a beautiful gown. He'll be in a tux. You guys'll be drinking champagne. You can't waste that opportunity, Jess."

"What opportunity?" Jessica yelped. A few heads turned their way. Jessica flinched and hunched her shoulders.

"A wedding hookup? *A one and done in the Plaza Hotel?*"

Amelia moved her hand in a circle as if trying to force Jessica to understand what she was saying.

"Bradshaw."

Jessica felt the blood drain from her face when Hayes approached their table. She tipped her head to see over his shoulder, as if she could somehow tell what direction he had come from. If he had overheard what her sister had just said. Forcing herself to drag her gaze back to him, she willed her banging heart to calm down.

"Hayes." She tipped her head. He hesitated. Probably wondering if she was giving him shit about his name again.

"What're you doing here?"

"Having coffee with my sister." She smiled sweetly. "What are *you* doing here?"

When he didn't answer her immediately, she looked toward the counter, the line there. She didn't see anyone he might have been there to flirt with, so she couldn't tease him about that.

"Met Ezekiel earlier for coffee."

The mayor. Well, hell, she couldn't give him shit about that. Hayes would pay for bougie coffee to meet with the mayor.

"Nice." She nodded.

"We still on for Saturday?" He took a step back and shoved his hands in the pockets of his Carhartt coat.

"Saturday?" she mumbled. *What the hell was Saturday?* As far as she knew, it was just another day of filling her hours with necessary errands and household chores before going to work.

"Cooperstown," he reminded her.

"Oh." She nodded, willing her face not to burn, aware that Amelia was just across the table watching her with big eyes and soaking up all the conversation like a sponge. "Yeah, sure. I guess I thought we were going Sunday."

From the corner of her eye, she saw Amelia open her mouth to say something. Hayes cut her sister off with a wink.

A wink?

Hayes Kelley knew how to wink?

"Nah. We'll have more time if we go Saturday. And you'll still be home to do brunch with your family."

She considered flipping him the bird. Again. He would laugh. They had been comfortable enough with each other to be sarcastic and flippant for several years now. She would never have dreamt of mouthing him when she was waitressing under him. Now that he knew she wasn't scared of him, he seemed to like the verbal sparring.

"Great." She nodded. "Can't wait."

"Hey." He pulled a hand free of his pocket and gestured at her coffee. "You want a scone? Cinnamon roll?"

"No, thanks."

"My treat."

He was getting even with her for the Christmas tree. Being flirty, okay being *nice*, in front of Amelia.

"No, thanks, Hayes. I'm good."

"Okay." He turned to Amelia with a smile. "See ya, Amelia."

Amelia lifted her chin to return his smile and then twisted around to watch him walk out.

"So. You were saying." She turned back to Jessica with a pointed look.

"No, I wasn't. You were rudely implying—"

"Oh, no." Amelia shook her head. "Nothing rude. And not implying. Just saying I think you should take him for a ride. He's pretty hot."

Jessica snorted. "He's *not hot*. He's my boss."

Amelia shrugged.

"He looks like he crawled out from under a rock."

"Bullshit." Amelia sipped her drink. "He's hot. And you know it."

Jessica cleared her throat. "So. Did you think of anything to get Mom and Dad for Christmas?"

"See?" Amelia pointed her finger at Jessica. "Dodging. Refusing to discuss. Just admit it. Admit that you think he's hot, and we'll move on."

"How are you the bossy sister? I'm older than you."

Amelia started humming the theme song from the TV game show *Jeopardy*.

"I'm not bossy. And I like Hayes. You've never had a nice thing to say about Nolan."

Jessica flinched. "Okay." She sighed. "Yeah. Hayes is hot. And Nolan's..." She stared at her sister, desperate for something to say about her boyfriend. "Tall."

"Tall?" Amelia laughed and rolled her eyes.

"Yeah, like, tall, dark, and..."

"You can't even say it when you don't mean it." Amelia groaned. "I think we should get Mom and Dad a new microwave."

"What?"

"They need a new one."

"That's such a boring present."

"But something they need. They wouldn't want us to spend a lot on something they don't need."

Jessica snorted and rolled her head on her neck. "No wonder you like Hayes. You sound just like him."

CHAPTER 14

*H*ayes

She was talking as she pulled her door open.

"I can drive."

Over her shoulder, Hayes spotted sections of an artificial Christmas tree spread over the living room floor. Boxes of ornaments were scattered over the sofa and chair.

"No." He stepped inside and surveyed her mess. "Tornado blow through here last night?"

"I'm decorating."

Hayes shook his head as he swung around to look at her. "Is that what you call it?"

She poked him in the gut and narrowed her eyes at him.

"Move your truck," she told him. "I'll drive."

"No." He gave her a once-over, regretting it immediately. He had only wanted to make sure she was ready to go, but her black skinny jeans, buffalo plaid shirt, and black boots did something to his insides. Roasted them. Afraid if he spoke again, steam or ash would come out of his mouth, Hayes gave himself a second to breathe. "I'll drive."

"Why?"

"Because my truck is in the way." He gave her a wide-eyed stare and arched his eyebrows.

"So, move it."

"Bradshaw." He drew in a deep breath and closed his eyes. "Are you ready to go?"

"I need to brush my teeth."

He blinked and nodded. "Go do that. I'll be waiting."

She eyed him suspiciously for a second. "Don't go getting any ideas about putting my tree together for me."

Hayes lifted his hands, palms out, as if to plead innocence. "I'll do what I can to hold myself back."

She rolled her eyes at his sarcasm, but he knew her well enough to know she was fighting a grin. When she finally turned and walked back down the hallway, Hayes made sure not to watch her. Instead, he stuffed his hands in his pockets again and wandered around the living room looking at her decorations. He hadn't been to Jessica's house often. He had dropped things off or picked things up a few times through the years. But he had never actually come inside for a visit until the other day when he dropped by and roped himself into being her wedding date. He had never seen her house decorated for any holiday. Now that he was here, surrounded by her things, he was curious.

The tree was probably a six-footer. He eyed the ceiling and then looked back at the sections of the tree on the floor. The house was small; she couldn't possibly put up a bigger tree than that. Unless she bent the top half over. Her decorations seemed to include every color in the rainbow, as compared to the tree she and Capri had decorated at the Chop House. That one was done in all blues and silvers. It was elegant, Hayes supposed, and he liked it. But for a moment, he had an itch to see her tree here at her house all finished and sporting reds and greens and golds as well as the blues and silvers at the restaurant. Did she have homemade ornaments? Things she and her sister had made when they were in school?

The tree when he was a kid was like that—covered in the colored bells and lights found in department stores, but his mom had saved all his goofy looking angels and gingerbread men, and she hung everything on the tree. Even when he was in high school. When he was a teen, the homemade ornaments had embarrassed him. Now, he wondered what had become of them. Probably still packed away in his parents' attic.

"Ready?"

He snapped his attention to Jessica as she appeared again with a short wool coat tossed over her shoulder and her purse in her hands. She dropped her phone inside the black bag but held onto her keys. Hayes eyed them warily, but he said nothing.

"Let's go." He led her out the front door, breathing a silent sigh of relief when she locked the door behind her and dropped her keys in her bag.

"Why didn't you want me to drive?" she asked him as he nodded for her to walk ahead of him to his truck.

There wasn't a reason. Other than the fact that his truck was parked in her driveway and moving it just so she could drive seemed like an unnecessary hassle.

"No reason."

She eyed him silently over the hood of the truck as she made her way around it to her side. Once settled in the cab with the engine running, Jessica plopped her purse on the floor at her feet and dug her phone out. Hayes eased out of her driveway and slowly pulled into the street.

"So, did Amelia tell your parents we're going to Cooperstown today?"

She narrowed her eyes at him. "No. Your evil plan didn't work."

"My evil plan?" He thumped his fist on his chest. "I didn't do anything."

"Just remember. If you get people riled up about this wedding date thing, they're gonna give you shit about it, too."

"I didn't do anything!" he repeated.

"How's your dad?" she asked him a few minutes later.

"Good. He's meeting his old cronies at the diner for breakfast this morning."

"Yeah? Who's he hang out with?"

"Eh." Hayes squeezed one eye closed to concentrate. "Larry Konrad. Mike Loos. And a few other guys I don't know."

"That's nice."

Hayes glanced her way to find her smiling at him. No trace of sarcasm or irritation. She meant it; she was glad his dad had guys to hang out with. But as far as Hayes knew, that was Jessica. True, she could be a thorn in his side, but she loved it. And honestly, he did, too. But she was a compassionate, giving person with everyone.

"What're you—?" He frowned when she tapped a button on the radio screen.

"I'm not riding to Cooperstown and listening to the news the whole way."

"Oh, no." Hayes groaned.

"Or the Foo Fighters. Do you have Sirius XM?"

"Mm." He kept his answer purposely noncommittal. Not to be deterred, she tapped the screen again, found the apps, and selected Bluetooth. "What're you doing?"

"Finding us some good music to listen to."

"Did you just—? Did you—?"

Jessica sat back in her seat, eyes on her phone as she scrolled. Hayes peeked at her as he drove—careful to watch the road—and saw her eyes light up. Some lively, fun sounding Christmas song started.

"Shoot me." He groaned.

"It's Kelly Clarkson. Who doesn't like Kelly Clarkson?"

He did. But dammit, he hated to admit that to her.

"I think you need a little Christmas cheer."

"If by cheer you mean a cold beer, I think you're right."

"It's not even eight in the morning."

"Lunch time." He shrugged.

"Do you have any siblings?"

Her out of the blue question took him by surprise.

"No. Why?"

She rested her head on the seat and closed her eyes.

"Because I can't imagine a world with two of you."

CHAPTER 15

*J*essica Hayes grumbled at a few of her song choices on the drive, but he never seemed too out of sorts over any of them. Jessica wouldn't swear to it, but a few times she thought she saw him tapping his fingers to the rhythm on his steering wheel. She wondered if he regretted driving; if they were in her car, would he take control of the music selection? Or would he let her have her way?

Once in Cooperstown, Hayes seemed game to follow her around as she strolled down the quaint streets looking through the windows of boutiques and bookstores. Once or twice, he reminded her they were looking for a wedding gift. Jessica simply stuck her tongue out at him and reminded him that she needed to Christmas shop, too.

Eventually, she hit the jackpot at a home décor boutique. Hayes had followed her inside each and every store she had ducked into, hands in his pockets, deadpan expression on his face. If she asked for his opinion on something, he gave it begrudgingly. Sometimes he added an eye roll.

But when she found the black Waterford crystal martini glasses, he had to arch his eyebrows. Hayes was tight with his money, but he also appreciated the finer things when it came to his bar at the restaurant. Of course, the Waterford martini glasses would appeal to him. For the bar.

"I think so," she said, eyes on the glasses again. "They're beautiful."

Another grumble from behind her.

"I mean, even if you don't drink martinis, they're beautiful."

"Sure, if you wanna part with that much money for glasses they'll likely never use."

Jessica turned slowly and narrowed her eyes at him. "It's a wedding gift. No one uses their wedding gifts."

Hayes answered with a dramatic shrug. "So spend twenty bucks instead of three hundred and twenty."

"Oh my God," she muttered. "You are impossible."

"Does this mean I have to buy lunch?" he asked as she selected two of the glasses.

"You can now, yes," she answered as she led him to the small counter at the back of the boutique. "And you know what? I am really hungry."

"Ouch." He sighed. "I've seen you slam burgers when you're not hungry."

If they weren't in a fancy little space, surrounded by expensive crystal and two snooty-looking ladies, Jessica would have laughed out loud. Instead, she snorted softly and shook her head as she pulled her credit card from her card case.

She glanced at her watch as the woman behind the counter wrapped the glasses in tissue paper. "What time do we need to head back? Did I take too long? Will you still have time to get a burner ordered for your dad?"

"We have the night off, so we can take as long as you want."

"What?" She turned to him with a severe frown.

"Capri is playing the role of Jessica Bradshaw tonight. And Kyler Tremont will be Hayes Kelley."

"Why?" She tipped her head. "You don't have to buy me lunch."

Hayes shrugged as if to blow off her question.

"We are going back home tonight." She arched her eyebrows. "Right?"

As if he could read her mind, Hayes simply gaped at her.

"And we thank you for stopping in." The older woman's voice drew her attention away from Hayes. She turned as the woman stepped out from behind the counter and handed the shopping bag over to her.

"Thank you," Jessica said sincerely. The bag wasn't particularly heavy, but when Hayes reached for it, she let him take it.

"I thought it would be a good chance to test Capri and Kyler. We're gonna be gone a few nights for this damned wedding," he reminded her.

"You don't have to go with me." She peeked up at him as they carefully wound their way back through the crystal displays in the shop. Hayes visibly shuddered when they stepped back out on the sidewalk.

"I'm going with you," he told her. "And tonight will be a good chance to see how things run without us."

"Things will run fine without me," she mumbled.

"You know that's not true," he argued. "You're the brains in there, Bradshaw."

She glanced at him again as they walked. "I do like being the brains," she admitted. "But it's all your vision. I follow your orders."

"You don't really believe that, do you?"

She didn't. When she had first taken on the role of restaurant manager, she had followed his orders, worked to fulfill his vision. But Hayes had always been interested in her opinion, her thoughts.

"No. But still. You're the boss."

"Let's get lunch first," he suggested. "We can hit one of the bigger appliance stores on the way out."

"Okay."

"And I promise I will have you home in plenty of time to do brunch tomorrow with your family."

She laughed softly.

"What're you gonna do about Nolan?"

"What *can* I do about Nolan? My sister's bangin' him. I hope she's at least getting the full experience there."

"You don't think he's—you don't think—?"

She tipped her head back to look up at him with a grin.

"I have no idea." She couldn't hide her amusement. "Pretty hard to judge that just by looking at someone, isn't it?"

Hayes made a show of looking her up and down. "If you say so."

She quirked an eyebrow at him and shook her head. "I'm just lookin' out for my sister. The guy's only with her for one reason. I just hope she's enjoying herself, too."

"How do you know that?" he asked.

"How about here?" She pointed her thumb at a pub.

"You picked it for the fake snow in the windows, didn't you?"

"No. I picked it because that Stella Artois sign is calling my name."

He gave her a wry grin and pulled the door open for her. Jessica stopped just inside the door, Hayes close enough to her when the door closed behind them, she could almost feel him pressed against her.

"Two?" A young blond guy appeared at the host's stand.

"Yes, please."

The kid grabbed two menus and nodded for them to follow him to a two-top table far enough away from the door that people entering or leaving wouldn't make them cold. As he walked away, Hayes shrugged out of his coat and hung it on the back of his stool. He pushed his menu aside as he sat down.

"What're you getting?" she asked him. Hayes watched her hang her purse on the stool, unzip her coat, and slip out of it. He flinched a bit when she hung it up on the stool, but Jessica couldn't make out what he was thinking, and he didn't say anything.

"Burger."

She sat down and opened her menu.

"You?"

"One of everything," she answered, eyes still on the menu.

When she peeked at him, she caught him with a grin on his face. The waitress appeared a few seconds later; Jessica was still focused on the menu.

"Hey." The girl sounded happy without being bubbly. Hayes would appreciate that. "What can I get for you to drink?"

"Do you have any of the Harvest Hues Amber Ale left?"

"Tap Meister Brewery?" the girl scrunched her face up in thought. "I think so."

"Two, please," Hayes told her with a nod. Jessica closed her menu and tipped her head at him. "One's for you. Unless you were serious about a Stella Artois."

CHAPTER 16

*H*ayes

"So." Jessica swallowed a fry and wiped her hands on a napkin. "When we're done here, we find an appliance store to get a burner or order a burner for your dad's stove."

"That's the plan." Hayes nodded as he polished off the last of his burger.

"And then? What? We go back home?"

"Unless you have something else you need to do."

"I don't," she said quietly with a quick shrug. "It's just... We'll be home in time to work."

"Yep." He nodded. "And yet, we're not going to work."

"That's bizarre," she whispered.

"Taking a night off?"

"You. Taking a Saturday night off. When you'll be right there. I don't think I've ever seen you do that."

Uncomfortable under her heavy stare, Hayes swept his gaze around the mid-scale bar. It was nothing like the Chop House, and yet, it was a completely different level than a greasy spoon tavern. Hayes had been here before, years ago. Most likely, the place had been under different ownership then. He didn't always want a place like the Chop House. In fact, he rarely ate in upscale, foody restaurants with high dollar menus. If the food was good, he would gladly sit in a dive and knock back a beer or two with a meal.

He didn't miss work, though. Ever. Funny, for a guy who used to cut school like he was a professional butcher. Hell, some days he wondered how he even graduated high school. He and his buddies skipped class more days than they attended, and half the time he was in school, it was the in-school-suspension room, rather than one of his classrooms.

He'd cleaned up his act, though, by the time he went to college. Mainly because he had to pay for that out of his own meager bank account. He knew better than to expect his parents to help him out, after the way he blew off his high school years. Hayes was a smart guy; he might have earned some scholarship money if he had worked harder. Hell, if he had just shown up more.

As it was, he got an associate degree. Took a few business classes. And then worked out a deal to buy the restaurant after all the years he had worked there. Thankfully, it had all worked out.

"Nothing better to do," he mumbled.

His buddies still lived in the area. Well, some of them did. But most of them were married. Some had little kids now. And Hayes had no interest in trying the dating thing again. Lisa had broken something inside him. Bad enough to make him hurt and then bad enough to make him not give a damn anymore once the hurt scarred over and he found himself getting through weeks and then months without thinking about her.

When he glanced at Jessica, she was watching him with a thoughtful frown.

"What?"

"Just thinking." She picked up her beer, only to hold it while she studied him. "Have you ever closed the Chop House?"

Hayes let out a frustrated sigh and nodded. He had. And he didn't want to talk about it.

"Oh, God." She cringed and reached over the table with her free hand to touch him. Rather than look her in the eyes, Hayes watched her small hand cover his and pat it just once before she drew it away. "I'm sorry. I'm an idiot."

The only time he had closed the Chop House was when his mom died. Her funeral had been on a Saturday morning. There had been no way in hell he wanted to shuck that damned suit and tie and change into anything other than a bottle of high proof whiskey and his sheets and wallow away the nightmare of losing a parent. They had survived it, he and his dad. And yet, Hayes lived every day wholly aware that he would have to do it again one day. Alone.

Hayes simply shook his head now. Jessica had been there. Hell, he remembered the day his mom had been diagnosed with cancer. He had come in to work with the fucking rock of Gibraltar on his shoulders, ready to kill the first dumb ass who looked at him wrong. Jessica had seen the look on his face and cornered him. Guided him to his office and gone to get him a shot of tequila. He had argued, told her his tequila was for sipping, not slamming. Rather than cowering from him, she had shoved him back to sit at his desk, got in his face, and ordered him to drink it. Once he had thrown it back, she locked his office door and leaned against it with her arms folded over her chest and ordered him to talk.

Hayes cleared his throat. Jessica had been there every day he had. She knew the days his mom struggled almost as intimately as he did. Because she had always asked about her, always checked on his dad, and always asked after him, if he needed anything. She'd been at work when his mom died, though he and his dad had been with his mom. Jessica had been at his mom's funeral.

"I'm sorry," she mumbled again. "That was completely insensitive of me."

He grunted in reply. Bradshaw couldn't be insensitive if she tried. Sometimes, people didn't think before they spoke. And to be fair, that was the one and only time he had ever closed the restaurant down. And when the Chop House was open, he was there. Hayes understood her surprise about tonight.

"So." He fiddled with the ketchup bottle on the table. Hayes wasn't a rainbow surfing sort of guy, didn't need unicorns and fluffy clouds to make his day. But he didn't want to sit here and think about his mom, to make Jessica feel bad for what she had said. Might as well change the subject. "You think Nolan is only seeing your sister for sex."

The way Jessica blinked at him, confused by the jump in conversation topics, almost made him laugh. He couldn't help the smile. As if she finally caught up with him, finally realized he didn't want to discuss his mom, she laughed and shook her head, finally taking a drink.

"I do, yes."

"Why?"

"Whaddaya mean why?"

"Convince me." He drilled her with a hard stare.

"You don't think—"

"Pretend I don't know Amelia or Nolan. I'm one of Rex's groomsmen. Convince me."

"Um." Jessica frowned and pursed her lips. "The likelihood of me talking about my sister's sex life with one of Rex's groomsmen is about the same as the likelihood of aliens taking over the world tomorrow."

"Time's ticking." He took another drink.

"Hayes. She's twenty-five. She's gorgeous. Just the right balance of slender and curves. Beautiful smile. And she's fun. What else would a guy his age want with her?"

"You say *his age* like thirty-five is ancient." He pointed and narrowed his eyes at her. "How old do you think I am?"

"Yeah, but are you banging my sister?"

The harsh bark of laughter surprised him. Jessica drew back and arched her brows at him.

"What was that? Did you just laugh? Like, really? Laugh?

"I am not banging your sister," he announced. "I don't want to bang your sister. But you just said all these wonderful things about her. Why wouldn't he want to be with her because of those things? She's fun, remember?"

"She's just a kid—"

"Do you think he deflowered her?"

Jessica hesitated, as if he had taken her by surprise again.

"What?" he coaxed her. "I *do* have a large vocabulary."

"Pardon me if I'm only used to hearing the adults' only version of your large vocabulary."

"Well?" He tipped his head dramatically.

"No."

"And how old were you?"

"How—? What?"

"How old were you? The first time?"

She pressed her lips together and studied him with an intense expression, like she was trying to decide how much to say.

"Eighteen," she finally mumbled.

"And you think that your sister waited? And she's a sweet little innocent girl? And Nolan's taking advantage of her?"

"You're supposed to be on my side," she said softly.

"Jess." Hayes took a deep breath and flopped back on his

stool. "Look, all I'm saying? You and I are here hanging out, right? Havin' a reasonably good time?"

"Did you just say you're having a reasonably good time with me?" She narrowed her eyes. "You've known me for ten friggin' years, and you can't even admit that I'm fun?"

Again, the smirk on his face was there without his brain's permission.

"Okay, sure. You're fun. You're pretty. You're smart. You think everyone in here is looking at us and thinking we're sleeping together? That I'm taking advantage of you?"

"That's different."

Hayes couldn't swear to it, but her cheeks appeared flushed.

"What if he's a nice guy? So he was married, and things didn't work out. What if his wife cheated? Or what if they just realized they didn't have enough in common to stay together? What if she won't let him see his kid? So now he's thirty-five and alone. And he meets Amelia and he's attracted to her? Sure, for her body, but for her smile. Her wit. Her sense of adventure."

"I have no sense of adventure, do I?" She propped her chin in her hand and stared at him a bit pathetically.

"What?" He shook his head. "No. No, this isn't about you. I'm just saying maybe you're being too hard on Amelia. On Nolan. Maybe he loves her."

Jessica sighed and lifted her glass to swallow the last of her beer.

"Could be fun," she mumbled. Hayes took a deep breath. She had only had two beers. But they were both sixteen ounces and higher ABV. Higher alcohol by volume meant someone on the thin, quiet, don't-drink-a-lot side, could feel the effects of said alcohol much quicker than someone like him.

What the hell did she mean could be fun?

The last thing he had said was that thing about everyone in here thinking they were sleeping together.

"What could be fun?"

He shouldn't have asked. Jessica wasn't bombed, but she was tipsy. Hayes should be the gentleman and pack her up, get her to the truck, and finish the business of the day to get her home.

"The wedding," she answered simply. "I mean, we do have fun together. It wouldn't have to suck, ya know? You being my date for the wedding."

Hayes threw his head back and howled a laugh that drew a few stares.

"Let's go." He slid off the stool and grabbed his coat.

"I'm not drunk," she told him. "One more and I could be. But I'm not."

"Okay." He nodded as he watched her take her coat from her stool and attempt twice to slide her arm into the sleeve. Both times, she spun around and missed. "Let me help."

She laughed softly as he helped her slip the wool coat on, grabbed her purse, and stepped in front of him when he made to usher her out.

"Thanks for lunch, Kelley."

CHAPTER 17

Jessica

Damn Hayes. Now Jessica found herself watching Nolan, watching the way he interacted with her sister. If she wasn't careful, Amelia might think she had changed her mind, that she wanted Nolan to take her to the wedding.

He had grabbed her a bottle of water at the appliance store. Without asking if she needed one. As far as she knew, she hadn't stumbled around like a drunk. Just mumbled that little thing about how it could be fun, and yes, if she were being honest, she would have to admit that the two beers she drank were the only reason those words had come out of her mouth.

Hayes had found a kid in the kitchen appliances and told him what he needed. Good thing Hayes knew what he was talking about, because the kid working there looked like he was ten and more familiar with video game consoles than appliances used for cooking. Hayes had been prepared with a brand name, a model number, and a serial number, and had almost scooted the kid right out of the way in front of the computer. Jessica had nibbled on her lip the entire time Hayes looked at the parts schematic, because she was afraid she would laugh if she didn't. The part had to be ordered, but at least the company would ship it directly to him.

Although, as they walked away from that department, Jessica found herself thinking she wouldn't have minded a trip back to Cooperstown with Hayes.

When they left the store through the main doors, he grabbed a candy bar in the checkout lane and a bottle of water from the cooler in front of it. He had offered her the first bite of the candy bar, and she had gladly accepted, happy the water and drive helped clear her head.

"How's your mimosa?" Amelia leaned into her now and nodded at the cranberry mimosa in front of her.

"Good."

Amelia and Nolan had both ordered a bloody mary. Jessica had never seen her little sister drink a bloody mary in her life, but she had channeled Hayes and reminded herself that Amelia did like tomato juice, and vodka was often her first choice for a cocktail.

"Wanna try it?" Amelia picked up her glass. Jessica turned her nose up at the stalk of celery sticking out the top of the glass.

"No. Thanks."

"Want my olive, Mel?" Nolan asked her. He held his hand out, the olive there in offering.

"Thanks." Amelia plucked it from his hand and tossed it in her mouth. "How was your shopping date?"

"You had a date, Jess?" Their mom asked from across the table.

Jessica considered kicking Amelia, but she chose the high road and elbowed her instead.

"No. I didn't have a date. Went to Cooperstown yesterday to go shopping."

"With Hayes."

"What?" Mom's eyebrows and ears perked up at Amelia's announcement.

"Not a big deal. I needed to get Chelsea's wedding gift. Not like there's a lot of places to buy something like that here in Holly Creek."

"They have a beautiful Christmas wreath on display right now at the craft store," Mom argued. "Chelsea would love it."

They did, and Chelsea would. However, Jessica wasn't sure big city people did crafty, country-looking holiday decorations in their apartments and townhouses. She had no doubt Chelsea and Rex's place would be gorgeous, but she didn't think for a second that wreath or anything else she bought here in Holly Creek would match their décor.

"Anyway, Hayes had to order a burner for his dad's stove. So we went together."

"That's nice." Mom nodded and sipped her own mimosa. "He takes good care of his dad."

Jessica had to agree. Didn't sound like Hayes or his dad ever got too sentimental, but it was obvious they cared about each other. Still, thinking of the two of them home alone, eating chili and watching football, for Christmas, made her a little sad.

"Did he get a burner ordered?" Dad asked.

"Yeah."

"And did you find something for Chelsea?"

"I did." Jessica didn't want to discuss what she had paid for the gift, so she didn't particularly want to discuss the gift itself.

"And did you guys go out? In Cooperstown?" Amelia asked.

Leave it to Amelia to reroute a discussion right into an oncoming train.

"We had lunch before we came home." Jessica hoped she sounded innocent. Because lunch had been innocent. Even if they had sort of discussed sex. And even if she had sort of had too much to drink. Certainly nothing had happened, and she didn't want her sister teasing her about Hayes in front of their parents.

"Carla, that looks good." Nolan cut loose with a whistle as their waitress approached with part of their order. The woman winked at Nolan as she put the plate of waffles piled high with whipped cream in front of Jessica's mom.

"It is good." Carla pointed her fork at Amelia's boyfriend. "Told ya you should order it."

"Nah." He shook his head with a sheepish grin. "Watching my figure."

Amelia snorted. Jessica watched her sister lean into Nolan and say something quietly enough that no one else could hear them. Nolan's answering smile seemed warm and sincere. The waitress moved around the table to set Amelia's breakfast burrito down and then slide Jessica's French toast in front of her.

"Be right back, gentlemen."

"Eat." Nolan waved his hands at them. "Eat it while it's hot."

Amelia dove in immediately. Their mom cut a strip off her waffles. Jessica studied her plate for a moment, remembering her conversation with Hayes the day before.

He had commented on Amelia's sense of adventure. Amelia who was drinking a bloody mary and eating a burrito instead of having the traditional mimosa and French toast breakfast Jessica was having.

"What's wrong?" Amelia nudged her.

"Nothing." She looked up with a smile, though again, she

felt a little wave of sadness. "I'm going to use the restroom. Be right back."

She felt her family's eyes on her as she crossed the restaurant to the restrooms. Damn Hayes for making her think. No, wasn't his fault. In fact, he had been the voice of reason yesterday about her sister. But Jessica liked her life the way it was. Maybe boring, steady, and in a rut was her future.

Depressing, she decided as she ducked into a stall to use the restroom. The outside door opened while she was still in the stall. Before she could wonder who it was, Amelia started talking.

"Did he kiss you?"

"What?" Jessica flushed the toilet, arranged the tail of her shirt the way she wanted it, and unlocked the door. Amelia stood with her butt resting on the counter, so Jessica had to push her out of the way to wash her hands.

"Did Hayes kiss you?"

"Why would he kiss me?" Jessica rolled her eyes. Damned if it wasn't an intriguing thought, though. She had a flash of his face in her mind—his thick eyebrows, dark eyes, and that damned delicious-looking stubble on his face. *Imagine covering that in whipped cream or syrup and licking it off.*

Stunned by the thought, the idea, by what that idea did to her body, Jessica ducked her head and leaned in to wash her hands.

"Why wouldn't he?"

"Because he's my boss," Jessica reminded Amelia. "And it's not like that with us, anyway. We're friends."

She snatched a couple of paper towels so violently a few flew off the pile on the counter and drifted to the floor.

"It's not like you guys're cops. Like you're partners and being intimately involved would be a bad thing for your safety. And it's not like you guys work at some big corporation where he could get in trouble for sexual harassment." Amelia shrugged. "I totally think you should sleep with him."

Jessica dried her hands and tossed the paper towels. "Mel, you're worrying me."

"What do you mean?" Amelia shifted and straightened as she moved away from the counter.

"Why the sudden push for me to sleep with Hayes? Why does my sex life matter to you?"

Amelia grinned. "Lack of."

"Are you not getting taken care of? Nolan falling short in the bedroom?"

Amelia snorted and threw her arm around Jessica's shoulders. "He's hot, Jess."

"Yeah, I guess so," Jessica agreed, assuming Amelia meant Nolan.

"So what's stopping you?" Amelia asked as they returned to their table, where their parents and Nolan were all eating now. Jessica eyed her dad's buffalo chicken sandwich and then studied Nolan's Reuben. "Live a little, Jess. Promise it won't hurt."

CHAPTER 18

*H*ayes

He didn't turn around when the door closed behind him. Simply waited, the fingers of one hand curled around a cigarette and a Glencairn with a pour of bourbon in the other. Hayes wondered what Jessica had done with her Saturday night off. He had pulled into her driveway around three, so yes, they could have both gone to work. But, as he had told her, he needed to know someone else could man the show while they were in the city for the wedding.

There hadn't been time to talk during kitchen hours. Business was picking up; the holidays had a way of making people want to get out and be more social. Hell, even he had enjoyed being out on Saturday with Jessica.

Bradshaw. Best to think of her as Bradshaw. One of the guys.

Just one of the guys with those long, dark silken waves around her face. With the bright eyes and those thick lashes.

Don't even start on the blouse she's wearing tonight.

"I could get used to that night off," she announced as she climbed up to sit by him on the picnic table.

"Liar." He turned his head only slightly and stared at her boldly.

"You're right." She grinned.

"What'd you do?"

"Ate junk food. Took a bubble bath and had a glass of wine."

Hayes held his breath as he waited for her to say more. He couldn't sit here and talk to her with the image of her soaking in a tub with a glass of wine stuck in his head. He shifted on the table, bent his knees, and rested his feet on the seat. Looked like he was restless, when in actuality, he was worried his dick was about to tent his pants. Not a good look for a boss when he was talking to his employee.

"And watched some stupid movies." She took a drink and looked back at him, seemingly unaware of his personal struggle. That was a relief. "You?"

"Ate junk food," he answered. "And watched movies."

"No bubble bath?"

"I was out of bubbles."

The smirk on her face was worth his current discomfort.

"Do you know how to dance?"

"Do I what?"

"You heard me." She tipped her head. "C'mon, Hayes. We're going to have to dance at the reception."

He sighed. Technically, yes, he knew how to do a few dances. He'd gone to ballroom dancing lessons with his parents when he was a kid. Lisa had insisted he go to the very same classes with her. Since losing his dance partner, his love of the actual sport had completely dried up, and he had no idea if he remembered the steps.

"Okay, we're gonna have to figure this out." Jessica dipped her head and rubbed her fingertips over her forehead. "Starting tomorrow. Come to my house after breakfast."

"I get up at five," he told her, hoping to put her off. "And eat by five-thirty."

"'kay." She nodded, unfazed.

"What? You're gonna teach me to dance?"

"Yeah." She sighed. "We only have about three weeks left."

"I think we'll figure it out."

"Sounds like Capri and Kyler didn't have any trouble Saturday."

He had known they wouldn't. And yet, that knowledge, that trust, didn't make Hayes feel any better about being gone later in the month.

"Yeah, they did okay," he said with no enthusiasm. "What're you drinking? Is that water?"

He eyed her champagne flute and then jerked his gaze to hers.

"Tequila."

"You? You're drinking tequila? Why?"

"Why not?"

Hayes raised his eyebrows and shrugged. "Oh, nothing. Just never seen you drink tequila before in my life."

"Yeah, well, maybe you don't know everything about me, Hayes Kelley."

He frowned at her, but deciding he didn't want to tangle with her when she was wearing such a scowl on her face, he looked away.

"How was brunch?"

The intensity of the previous moment went up in smoke when she laughed softly.

"It was fine."

"Did you go to Flora's?"

"No. Mom wanted a mimosa. I wasn't going to argue with her."

"Do tell." He rested his elbow on his knee, propped his chin in his hand, and stared at her curiously. "What's up with the drinking?"

"Am I drinking too much? Is this an intervention?"

"No." He shook his head. "Of course not. I like it."

"You like it?"

"I get tired of drinking alone," he told her as he moved to clink his glass to hers.

"If you went to brunch tomorrow, what would you order?"

"Mmm." He sighed and smoothed his fingers down over his face. Probably should have shaved earlier. Two days' worth of stubble and scruff probably had him looking homeless. "Maybe French toast."

"Hmm." She nodded, as if she approved of his answer.

"Or maybe, like, an applewood smoked bacon chicken sandwich." He shrugged. "Guess it would depend on the day."

"Gotcha." She turned her head, surveyed the alley in front of them. Hayes took the opportunity to study her long, soft curls. The sparkly shit on her eyelids. Her lip gloss. She was bundled up in a different coat than she wore Saturday, this one longer, probably warmer.

"How was Nolan?"

Jessica drew in a long, dramatic sigh and finally looked back at Hayes with a small smile.

"Okay, I guess."

"Yeah?"

"I thought about what you said," she mumbled.

"Hmm. Because maybe I'm right?"

"Remains to be seen."

"You really want me to come over for dance lessons tomorrow?"

"I do." She nodded. "You're not really gonna show up at five, are you?"

"What if I do?"

"Dress warm. I won't be up until seven."

CHAPTER 19

*J*essica

The knock on her door came as she sipped her coffee and studied her tree. Her totally *naked* tree. At least she was dressed, and the tree sections were put together. She should have decorated it Saturday night. Or Sunday. But she had been tired, and since that Saturday night off was so rare, she had treated herself to some Jessica-time in the form of a bubble bath, a glass of wine, and a book. And then movies.

She was careful as she unlocked the door and pulled it open, so as not to spill her coffee. Hayes, looking like a total grouch, stood on her front porch, wearing his usual uniform of jeans that had seen better days, Carhartt coat, and the backwards ballcap over his scowling face.

"Got some of that for me?" he asked with a nod at the coffee cup she held.

"Yep." She waited for him to step inside and then closed the door. "You know where the kitchen is."

He grumbled something as he disappeared down the hall

to the kitchen. Jessica stared after him for a second but quickly turned her attention back to her tree. She loved Christmas. And decorating. And baking. She loved *all things Christmas*. So why couldn't she get moving and get this done? She should have asked Amelia to help her. She could still do that, she supposed. Amelia could come over after Jessica got off work tonight. It would be late, but it would still be fun. And Amelia was young; she could handle the later hours.

Jessica snorted when she realized what she had just been thinking. Amelia was young. As if Jessica was that much older.

"What're you snorting about?"

"Hmm?" She turned and looked at Hayes as he moseyed back down the hall to stand by her. He had taken his coat off, revealing a red and blue plaid flannel, buttoned up over a navy t-shirt. His big hands dwarfed her coffee cup. Jessica lifted her gaze to watch him take a sip. He had shaved, but she knew by the time he opened the Chop House later, he would be wearing that yummy five o'clock shadow again.

Yummy? Seriously? Thanks a lot, Amelia.

"The dance thing," he said with a sigh, eyes on her tree now. "Was that a bullshit ploy to get me over here and help you with your tree?"

"No, but that's not a bad idea." She pursed her lips.

"What's the big deal?" He narrowed his eyes as he finally realized she was playing Christmas music. "What the hell is this?"

"Bing Crosby, Scrooge." She rolled her eyes. "Ever heard of him?"

"Is this what we're dancing to?"

"No. I was trying to get in the holiday spirit to decorate."

"And you've made so much progress." His voice was thick with sarcasm.

"I usually do all colors on my tree here," she told him, as if he gave a damn what she did with her Christmas tree. Judging from the look on his face right now, she didn't want to know what he thought she could do with it. "But I'm wondering if I should do something different this year."

"Like what?"

"I dunno." She shrugged. "Any suggestions?"

"French toast."

"What?"

"Did you make me French toast?"

She laughed softly and shook her head. "Sorry. No. I have some Pop-tarts."

"Yeah, that's a close second, for sure," he agreed.

"When did you get funny?" she asked him.

"What colors are you thinking of?" He took another drink and directed his gaze back to the tree. "For your tree."

"Gold. Crème. And brown."

"You want me to be honest?"

"No, Hayes. Lie to me."

"Okay." He nodded. "Sounds wonderful."

She laughed and moved closer to the end table to put her cup down.

"Let me just..." She crossed the room again to where she'd left her phone and tapped her music app. Hayes blinked in the sudden quiet. She looked back at her phone and scrolled through her liked songs.

"What'd you decide on?" he asked as he wandered to the window and leaned closer to look outside. "Huh."

"Haven't yet," she answered. "And what?"

"I meant colors," he told her. "It's snowing."

"No way!" She looked at him again, but she couldn't see much beyond him.

"Tiny little flakes."

"That's cool. I was gonna ask Amelia to come over after work and help me finish the tree."

"*Finish* the tree," he repeated.

"And gold and crème and brown is what I decided."

"Because if I don't like it, it's bound to be classy?"

She shot him a quick grin. "Maybe."

"I like the tree you and Capri did at the Chop House."

"I do, too, but I don't want to look at your blue and silver tree all night at work and then come home and look at my blue and silver tree at home all day."

"Fair point."

He put his cup down and wandered over to stand by her. Jessica realized then that he'd taken his boots off in the kitchen. Maybe because it was snowing. Maybe because she wasn't wearing shoes and if he stepped on her when they were dancing, he might break her toes.

"What kind of music do you think they'll play?" she asked him.

"Um." He slipped his hands in his pockets and leaned closer to look down at her phone with her. "Ratpack, maybe. Big band. Jazz."

"So, no 'Baby's Got Back'?" She peeked up at him with a little grin.

"If we're lucky."

"Frank Sinatra?"

"Sure." He nodded.

Jessica only scrolled through her songs again. "But which song?"

"Bradshaw." He took her phone and met her eyes when she glared at him. "It doesn't matter. If we can dance to one song, we can dance to everything."

"Not if it's the tango."

"My ass will *not* be on the dance floor if they are doing the tango. So. Problem solved."

"What if they have a rock band or something? I mean, I don't know what this is gonna be like. I don't know Rex and his family that well. What if they have, like, Bob Segar there to play?"

"Pretty sure that won't happen, because I'm pretty sure he's either retired or getting ready to retire."

"Blake Shelton," she suggested.

"Not rock and roll," he answered with a shrug. "Again, problem solved."

"Yeah, but what if Rex's family knows some big country star. Can you two-step?"

"Actually." He tapped the screen and "Fly With Me" started playing in the living room. "I can, yes. Stick with me, Bradshaw. I solved all your problems here." He winked at her as he tapped the volume on her phone screen.

"Do you even like Frank Sinatra?" she asked him.

"I do, yes." He nodded. "And what I'm wondering right now is if you're scared of me."

"Scared of you?"

"Scared to dance with me." He shrugged and put her phone back on the bookshelf. "You're full of excuses."

"Am not," she argued.

"Then let's dance." He held his hand out to her, the grin on his face reminiscent of something she'd seen recently in a horror movie. Still, she put her hand in his, stepped closer, and lifted her chin to look him in the eyes when he slipped his arm around her waist. "What're we doing? The waltz?"

"Yeah, I guess." She nodded.

"Bradshaw?"

"Hmm?"

"Do you know how to dance?"

Eyes locked with his, she laughed out loud. "I do, but it's been a long time."

"When and why did you learn ballroom dancing?"

They were moving now, stepping around her small living area, Sinatra serenading them.

"College," she answered. "Dated a guy that had money. And went to a dance with him at some country club thing in his hometown."

Hayes stared at her for a moment. "And?"

"He was a jerk. That night went okay, but we didn't stay together long."

"Why was he a jerk?"

"Well, he was a snob. It made him mad that I wouldn't get manicures. That I refused to paint my nails. He didn't like the way I wore my hair. He hated that I wore cut-off denim around my apartment. His mom didn't approve of my midwestern up bringing. And his brother hit on me one night."

"Is that why you don't like Rex?" Hayes asked quietly. Jessica wasn't sure, but it felt a bit like Hayes had smoothed his fingers over her lower back. Like a gesture to comfort her.

"I guess it's why I don't *trust* Rex." She pressed her lips together and frowned, eyes now glued to his chest. "He seems nice enough. But it's just that whole mentality."

"What did his brother do?"

"Hmm?" She jerked her gaze up to meet his eyes. "Oh. He kissed me. Or he tried to. I turned away so he kind of got my ear."

Hayes offered her a small smile.

"My turn to ask a question." She tipped her head back and quirked an eyebrow at him. She had never been this close to Hayes Kelley. Oh, they'd bumped into each other a time or two on busy days at the restaurant, but not like this. Not constant contact. Not by choice. She didn't hate it. Up close like this, she noticed his blue eyes weren't really blue at all, but hazel. He smelled like cedar, fresh and crisp, and it was suddenly all Jessica could do to not suck in a big breath of Hayes Kelley.

Because that would be weird. And he would damn sure notice.

"Great." That deadpan expression again.

"When and why did *you* learn ballroom dancing?"

CHAPTER 20

*H*ayes
"It's not an interesting story."

"I'll be the judge of that." She slid her hand off his shoulder to pat his chest. Hayes didn't mind her hand on him— shoulder, chest, he was good with it. Which was probably not good. He shouldn't have signed up for this. No good would come of him being Jessica's plus one for Chelsea Calhoun's wedding. He and Jessica—*Bradshaw*—had been hanging out more lately, and he was seeing things he liked about her, things he hadn't noticed before. Like the fact that when she smiled big, he could see a chip in her bottom front tooth. When she was really amused by something, her laughter was loud and throaty, and it made Hayes wonder what other sorts of sounds she might make.

He gave himself a mental shake. She had been a kid when she had come to work for him.

"I'm waiting," she reminded him. Her voice was quiet, but her stare was bold, challenging.

"My parents used to take lessons." He shrugged. "I was

probably nine. Ten? My mom would insist that I go with them. And I always got dragged out to the floor to pair up with someone."

"Really?" She narrowed her eyes at him suspiciously.

"Yes, really."

"That's a whole lot of good info there, Hayes."

"Like what? That I was a mama's boy?"

"No." She shook her head, the expression on her face telling him that was the furthest thing from her mind. "First of all, I love that your parents took dance lessons. I'm fascinated, really, that Wilson Kelley could dance with me if I asked him to."

Hayes offered her a sardonic smile. "He's free the night of the wedding if you want to swap dates."

"I don't," she answered.

"He was grumpy about it. About dancing with Mom."

"Color me shocked."

Her sarcasm dragged a laugh up from deep inside.

"But Mom was in charge. He was over the moon for her, so even if he griped about something, he did anything she asked."

Jessica's lips tipped up in a sad smile. "That's beautiful."

"Not for a nine-year-old boy whose mother wants him to waltz with old ladies."

"Old ladies who were probably actually your age now."

Hayes laughed and nodded. "True. But when you're nine, and you'd rather be out riding your bike or playing a pick-up basketball game, having old lady boobs stuck in your face isn't all that exciting."

Jessica snorted. She dropped her head forward to rest on his chest. That laugh—the throaty one—and the smell of her shampoo or perfume nearly crippled him with desire. He hadn't felt this way for so long, Hayes had forgotten how good it felt. The awareness of an attractive woman. The banter. The laughter.

His dick liked her, too. Thankfully, there was space between them, and she wouldn't realize what her nearness was doing to him.

"I'm sure that changed for you."

"'Course. By the time I was twelve, I was all about the boobs."

He hadn't even seen bare boobs now in a few years, other than those on his television. While he wasn't one to shy away from looking his fill when movie scenes offered those views, he couldn't remember the last time his dick stirred while looking at any of them.

Desperate for something to get his mind out of the gutter —more specifically, Bradshaw's shirt—he looked around her room, noticed the bare tree, and suddenly realized the Frank Sinatra song had changed to a Christmas song by Bruce Springsteen. Something quite a bit louder and faster, and yet, neither of them had noticed.

"Why are we dancing to Bruce Springsteen now?"

Jessica laughed and stepped away from him. Relief and disappointment tore through him, but Hayes knew better than to roll with the disappointment. They needed to keep this professional. Hell, if Bradshaw knew the things he was thinking about her, she might backhand him. And he couldn't blame her.

"You don't like Springsteen?"

"Yes, I like Springsteen, but there's not gonna be any Springsteen music at this reception. That I can guarantee."

She snickered as she reached for her phone.

"It's just a list of liked songs," she told him.

Hayes took her phone from her and looked around the room again. "Where's the speaker?"

"There and there." She pointed at one on the bookcase and one across the room on an end table.

"Sonos sound system?"

"Yep."

"Nice." He nodded. "This all the music you have?" He waved her phone at her.

"Yeah. I mean, I have some other playlists."

"But no vinyls?"

"Vinyls," she repeated. "No. Do you? Have record albums?"

"Some. My dad didn't want any of them after Mom...died. I took their albums. And their record player."

She studied him silently for a moment. "And do you listen to them?"

"Sometimes. I left him the Christmas albums, though."

"Like, wait." She reached for him, brushed her fingertips over his chest again. The touch zinged through him, raced through his gut, and zapped his dick. "When? Like, when you get home from work, do you go straight to bed? Or do you listen to music then?"

"You know what you remind me of?" He folded his arms over his chest and frowned at her.

"What?"

"A kid who can't believe her teacher has a life outside of school."

"Well." She shrugged. "I've worked for you for ten years. And I don't know what you do outside of the Chop House. And hanging with your dad."

"If I'm tired, I shower and go straight to bed. But I usually need time to unwind."

"I get that."

"So I shower. Maybe have another pour of bourbon. In the summer, I might have a cold beer."

"And is that when you listen to records?"

"Sometimes."

"What's your favorite?"

"Of my parents' albums?" he asked and continued when she nodded, "either a 1968 album by Sinatra. It's called *Frank Sinatra Sings for Only the Lonely.* Or a John Coltrane album called *Blue Train.*"

She stared at him for a moment and finally smiled. "Nice."

She tapped her phone and another Christmas song started, this one back to the classics. Dean Martin singing "Marshmallow World."

"What're you doing?" he called when she put her phone down and padded down the hall to the kitchen.

"I'm hungry," she answered. Hayes followed her, found her leaning over with her head in the fridge, her sweet little ass sticking up in the air. Couldn't have been more enticing if there had been a neon arrow pointing at it. "Are you?"

"Yep." He turned away. "Want more coffee?"

"Yes, please."

Hayes couldn't get out of the kitchen fast enough. He took his time finding their cups in the living room. Looked at the boxes of ornaments spread all over the sofa and chair. When he saw a pack of the gold, crème, and brown bells she must have been talking about, he nudged it with his foot so he could get a better look. The idea sounded horrible to him, but he had to admit the bells were pretty.

And Hayes knew anything Jessica touched turned to gold.

CHAPTER 21

*J*essica

"Look." Amelia nudged Jessica with an elbow in her ribs.

"What?" Jessica turned to look at her sister.

The snow that had started the morning she and Hayes were dancing had continued for a couple of days, leaving Holly Creek looking like a winter wonderland. Just in time for the annual sledding competition. Mostly kids signed up for it, though there were always a few adults in the mix. Jessica and Amelia had taken a shot at it a few years back. Neither of them did anything too fancy; Jessica had gone down the big hill on a traditional flyer sled; Amelia had flown down the hill on a round disc. Her crash landing at the bottom had put an end to their fun that year.

"Is that Hayes?"

Jessica looked to where Amelia was pointing. Of course it was Hayes, and yes, Amelia knew it. Jessica reached out and shoved Amelia's hand down to her side.

"Yes."

Hayes was surrounded by kids, holding a traditional flyer sled, messing with a runner. Jessica just hoped he wasn't greasing it to make it go faster. The big sledding hill was a lot of fun, but it had proved dangerous a time or two. Luckily, when Amelia crashed all those years ago, she had only broken her wrist. But there had been a few serious injuries, one that resulted in the county having to trim back some of the lower hanging limbs of the trees at the bottom of the hill.

"How's it going with him?"

Jessica sipped her hot chocolate and gave her sister the side eye.

"Fine. We're the same as we always are."

"Liar."

Jessica shrugged innocently. "I manage his restaurant. He barks out orders all night. He's grouchy. We got together that one day last week to practice dancing."

Amelia's eyes lit up at the reminder.

"Mmm." She nodded. "That's right. You fixed him breakfast."

"I fixed breakfast. I was hungry."

"But you fed him, too."

Jessica sighed and shook her head.

"Nolan and I celebrated last night," her sister announced.

"I'm not sure I want to know."

"Why do you always have to make it about that?" Amelia groaned. "He took me to Cooperstown for dinner. We walked around and held hands and shared hot chocolate."

Jessica felt a twinge of guilt. "What were you celebrating?"

"Well, we've been dating eight months now," Amelia told her.

"Eight months?"

That surprised her. In a good way, she had to admit.

"Yeah. So we had planned to have dinner together for that.

But also, he got a raise. Which is nice because we're kind of talking about buying a house."

"Really?" Jessica arched her eyebrows. "Wow, Mel. I had no idea you guys were that serious."

"Because you don't like him."

"Look, I'm sorry I've been a pain about it. I think I just assumed he was after you for that body."

Amelia snorted. "Well, could you blame him?"

"Of course not."

"He's good to me, Jess. He loves me."

Jessica met her sister's gaze and nodded. "Okay. That's all I need to hear."

"Now to get you back in the dating game."

Jessica only shrugged and turned her nose up. "I don't have time for it."

"Let's go say hi to Hayes."

"Subtle." Jessica rolled her eyes, but she willingly walked with Amelia to where Hayes was still surrounded by several kids. Most of them looked young, and Jessica was reminded of Hayes' story of dance classes and having old lady boobs stuck in his face. She was smiling about it when Hayes saw them approach.

"Give you five bucks to take 'em all," he said over the tops of the kids' heads. He sounded grumpy, but she knew he was kidding.

"Hayes! Can I go now?" A kid bundled up in a brown Carhartt coat and a bright orange stocking cap launched himself at Hayes to get his attention.

"Hansen." Hayes nodded and pointed at the kid even as he turned to survey the rest of the group. "Shaffer. You two. You're up."

A short kid with a green stocking cap pushed through the crowd to stand closer to Hayes. Jessica watched with interest as Hayes nodded and the boys put their sleds down. The boys climbed on their sleds and looked at each other.

"Give him a push, Bradshaw." Hayes nodded at the kid he had called Hansen.

"Me?" she yelped.

"You." He nodded.

Jessica handed Amelia her hot chocolate and moved up to stand by the kid on the sled.

"Count of three."

"Wait." Jessica threw her hand up. Hayes hit her with that deadpan look. "On three? Or after three? That's important, right? In a race?"

He was trying to fight it, but she could see the hint of a smile on his face.

"On three."

"Got it."

She and Hayes leaned over the boys. Hayes counted to three, and each of them pushed the boys to get them started. Hayes walked over to stand by her, but he kept his eyes on the boys as their sleds zoomed down the hill, snow flying in their wake.

"Stick around," he told her, still not looking at her.

"What?"

"You heard me."

Unfortunately, Amelia heard him, too, and insisted they stick around and help Hayes with the sled races. The only plans Jessica had for the day were hanging out with Amelia and working at five, so she couldn't beg off because she was busy.

The boys adored Hayes. That much was clear immediately. And even with the gruff demeanor, it was obvious Hayes was enjoying himself. Jessica found herself even more drawn to Hayes the longer she spent with him and the kids.

Had he wanted kids? When he was engaged? Maybe he had

dreams of marriage and kids and being out here on this hill with his own sons and daughters. Of watching his own children at the Christmas pageant. Playing Santa to his little boy or girl.

She had never asked him. It had always seemed too personal to pry into his failed engagement, the wedding that didn't happen. She wondered what he would say if she asked him now.

After another hour in the snow and the cold, her toes frozen, she was thrilled when Hayes told the boys to head to the Chop House for pizza. Some of the kids picked up sleds and headed to Main Street. Hayes hauled two of the flyer sleds off the ground and glanced at her and Amelia.

"You guys comin'?"

"Yeah!" Amelia answered before Jessica could open her mouth. "Need us to do anything for you?"

"Yep. You can get the natives settled while I get the pizzas in the oven."

Jessica had assumed he was ordering pizza for them, but now she wondered. Was he serving them homemade pizza? It wasn't something on his menu, and yet, it was a Saturday afternoon, before dinner hours. And it was his place. He could do whatever he wanted.

At the Chop House, Hayes disappeared into the kitchen while Jessica and Amelia stripped their coats off, tossed them aside, and got the boys all settled at a table. A few of them had worn snowsuits out there on the hill, so there were coats and snowsuits and boots kicked off and thrown everywhere. Jessica was a little iffy on the boys having their boots off in the dining room, but she reminded herself this was Hayes' place.

She picked up a coat and hung it on a chair, but Amelia shook her head.

"What?"

"I've got this," she told her. "Go help Hayes."

Hayes Kelley didn't need help in the kitchen. But Amelia wasn't serious; she simply wanted Jessica in the kitchen with him. She rolled her eyes at Amelia, but she ducked into the kitchen and hollered at Hayes.

"Need help?"

"Can you get some plates and silverware out? Get enough for you and Amelia, too."

"Sure."

CHAPTER 22

*H*ayes

Hayes hadn't expected Jessica and her sister to stick around all afternoon. But he was glad they did. He had made the pizza crusts earlier in the morning, so when the boys were done on the hill, all he had to do was top them and pop the pizzas in the oven. Jessica had been zinging here and there, grabbing plates and silverware, taking the boys drinks, and talking and laughing as she did so. Hayes had heard both her and Amelia talking to the boys about the sledding races, the upcoming holidays, and what the new cool video games were this year.

While he had originally planned to join them in the dining room while the pizzas baked, Hayes lingered in the kitchen instead. He liked the kitchen; it had always been his sanctuary. But today, he stayed out of the dining room, because he loved the rise and fall of voices and laughter coming from the front of the place. The noise in the Chop House was totally different from the status quo, and Hayes liked it. Seemed like Jessica and Amelia were having fun, too.

Obviously, neither of them had children. And since they had moved to Holly Creek from the Midwest, they didn't have extended family here. Hayes rarely saw Jessica interact with kids. People brought their children to the Chop House on occasion, and Jessica did a good job of catering to those children, or smoothing things over for the parents if those children got a little loud or rambunctious. But he had never seen her talk and laugh with kids like she was now.

Did she want a family? Hell, Hayes didn't even know if she wanted marriage. They had talked about it that one night recently, and she had said she wouldn't want a big wedding. But did she want a future with someone? Jessica had dated plenty through the years. He had seen her in a crush stage. He'd seen her in love, he guessed. And he'd seen her mad enough to throat punch a few of the guys she had dated. But Hayes wasn't sure what she saw for herself five or ten years in the future.

While he didn't miss Lisa, while he hadn't spent the past several years depressed over being without a woman, he did hate the missed opportunity for a family. He had wanted kids. More than one, after growing up as an only child. He would have taken two boys, two girls, one of each—he had just hoped he would be a dad someday.

Hayes had grown up watching his mom in the kitchen, learning from her and then taking that hard-won knowledge and experimenting and finding new ways to cook meats and vegetables. He had spent a good deal of time outdoors with his dad, too. Sure, he had been a pain-in-the-ass troublemaker kid, but he wasn't always in trouble. He hadn't realized how much giving up the dream of being a dad hurt until he got involved in the community events for kids. Spending that time out there on the hill, watching the kids participate in the Oktoberfest activities—especially the wiener dog races—watching the little ones line up to see Santa Claus—it was a balm for that heartache. Those kids gave him just as much as he volunteered to them.

But walking away after those sorts of activities always reminded him, he was alone.

The ovens beeped as the kitchen doors swung open again. Christmas music was playing in the dining room. All modern stuff by artists the boys were familiar with. The music faded a bit as the doors closed. Hayes looked over his shoulder as he pulled an oven door open.

"Can I help?"

"Yeah." Hayes nodded as Jessica joined him at the oven and grabbed a giant mitt. Together, they pulled the two pizzas—one sausage, one pepperoni—from the oven, placed them on the stainless-steel counters, and grabbed cutters to slice them. "Let 'em sit for a minute."

She nodded at him.

"You made these. Didn't you?" she asked him.

He answered with a curt nod.

"I seem to remember you working at the Oktoberfest, too."

He volunteered every year, but he didn't bother to correct her.

"You like kids." She sounded surprised.

Hayes fixed his gaze on the pepperoni pizza in front of him. "They're alright. Long as I can shove 'em out of here and back to their parents when they're done."

He felt her eyes on him as he rolled the pizza cutter over the pie.

"You better be careful, Kelley," she said softly. Her word choice sounded like a warning, but her tone was soft and sweet. Hayes glanced at her curiously. "People are gonna see through that grouch act you do."

"'s not an act," he promised her in his best growly voice. Jessica laughed at him and got busy cutting the other pizza.

They served the boys. Amelia filled their glasses again. Jessica and Amelia sat together at a two-top table, talking quietly, while Hayes sat with the boys. Mostly, they talked about video games. Hayes had played some when he was a kid, but technology changed at such a pace, the games he played were probably dinosaurs to them. He pushed them to talk about hunting and sports. He knew a few of the boys—the Hansen kid, for sure—hunted with their dads. And two of the kids here played basketball for the elementary school team.

When the pizzas were demolished, Hayes shooed them all back outside and told them to check in with their parents. The sledding races were over, but a few of the locals were still braving the cold under little white tents, selling their wares. Some sold candied almonds and caramel corn; some sold craft items and Christmas décor. Hayes' mom used to love to fiddle around on these sorts of days, visiting with friends and stocking up on goodies and gifts.

"Thanks for your help." He nodded at Jessica and Amelia. "I'll see you tonight, Bradshaw."

"I'll help you clean up," Jessica told him as she stood.

"I'd stay, but I told Mom I would do a little shopping with her."

Hayes saw the look Jessica gave Amelia and wondered what it was about. Not that it mattered, he reminded himself. Maybe Jessica thought Amelia was lying and had plans to see Nolan instead.

"You don't have to help." Hayes shook his head.

"I have nothing else to do right now," she insisted.

Another pointed look passed between the sisters.

"Go home and decorate your tree."

"We did that the other night," Amelia said as she pulled her coat back on. "Thanks for lunch, Hayes. It was good."

"Anytime."

Amelia headed for the door where the boys were still tugging on boots and zipping coats. Hayes watched Jessica watch her sister leave and wondered what she was thinking. But she turned away quickly and started stacking plates. Hayes shoved his hands in his pockets and walked over to the boys. None of them were young enough to need his help, but they were young enough to get rambunctious and break things if they weren't supervised.

"Thanks, Mr. Kelley."

"Hayes," he grumbled. He had told that kid several times to call him Hayes. The kid argued back just as many times that his mom said he was to call Hayes Mr. Kelley. It was slightly amusing, and Hayes' mother had been the same way. But somehow, it felt different when he was the adult being addressed as mister. It made him feel old.

Spending so much time with Jessica Bradshaw had reminded him of how it felt to be young, happy. He didn't want to jump back into being that grouchy, old man. Not yet.

The boys headed out in a group, all of them calling goodbye and thank you. Hayes watched them go, wondering which of them would go home later to a home-cooked dinner. Which would play with siblings. Which would get up and go to church with his family tomorrow.

"Do you want kids?"

He didn't so much as flinch at Jessica's voice behind him.

"What in the world would I do with a kid?" he asked as he turned to face her. Hands in his pockets, he headed back to the tables where she was now gathering up cups. "When they're little, they're a bag of poop and boogers. When they're in grade school, they want things. Every damned thing on a store shelf. And in high school, they're walking, mouthy hormones."

He snatched at the napkins on the table and avoided Jessica's eyes. She followed him when he went back to the kitchen.

"It's not too late, ya know."

"Too late for what?" he asked her. Jessica put the stack of cups down and grabbed an apron. Rather than run the dishwasher for the few items they had to wash, she had already filled the sink with hot, soapy water. "I'll wash them."

"To have kids." She bumped her hip to his to keep him from the sink. "I've got it."

"Poop and boogers," he repeated.

"What are you? Like thirty-seven? Guys can father babies a lot later than it's safe for women to get pregnant."

"I'm thirty-five," he corrected her, his tone indignant. "And I don't want kids."

"You're kinda good-looking. Surely, there's a woman in Holly Creek or somewhere close who would be into you—"

Before he knew what he was doing, Hayes dropped his hands on her shoulders and spun her around. Soap suds splattered, and water dripped to the floor between them when she pulled her hands from the sink.

"Or you could adopt—"

Jesus. Still talking.

Hayes cupped her face in his hands, leaned forward, and smashed his lips to hers. Thankfully, the talking stopped. No more incessant chatter or advice about how he could still have kids. And yet, now, he was in a lip lock with Jessica Bradshaw. His restaurant manager. The same kid who used to cower every time he opened his mouth back when she first started waitressing for him.

Not the same, though. She had been stick thin when she

was eighteen. Now, with her warm lips pressed to his, all Hayes could think about was her ass in the air the other day when he'd found her with her head in her refrigerator. The slight swell of her breasts under her tops, the occasional peek at her skin, the curves of her breasts, when she dressed for summer.

She hummed.

Just as his brain was ready to kick his ass and shove her back to the sink so he could beat a retreat and hide in his office, she *hummed*. Just a soft, little mewling sound in her throat. Fuck if he could walk away from that.

CHAPTER 23

*J*essica Hayes Kelley's lips were warm and soft. Not what she might have imagined them to feel like if she had ever wondered about kissing him. Water and suds dripped to the floor, her hands frozen there between them. She wanted to rest them on his shoulders.

No, she didn't. She didn't want to *rest* anything right now. Jessica fought the urge to grab Hayes by the shoulders and pull him in close. Wrap her arms around his neck and drag her fingers—suds and all—up through his hair. Shove that damned hat to the floor.

As if he could read her mind, he swept his mouth over hers again, and then slipped his tongue between her lips. Afraid to move, afraid they would both *find* their minds and snap out of whatever this was, Jessica parted her lips. His tongue sought hers—no other way to say it. Hayes Kelley was kissing her. *Kissing* her.

French kissing her.

His rough, calloused fingers held her face gently, as he

stroked his tongue over hers once and then twice. Jessica tasted the pizza they had both eaten, but more than that, she tasted Hayes. And she wanted more. When he broke that kiss, a soft little sob escaped her lips, but he had only stopped to breathe. When he kissed her again, he moved his hands, and Jessica thought to miss them, to miss his touch on her face. And then they were on her hips, and he was yanking her in close to him.

She reached for him and curled her wet fingers around fists full of his flannel shirt. Maybe he liked it or maybe she had pulled his chest hair—she didn't even know if he had chest hair—but his growl in response sent a shiver up her spine.

Was he into her?

Was she into him?

Jesus, what had Amelia seen that she had overlooked?

He dug his fingers into her hips and hauled her up against his middle. Against an erection the likes of which she hadn't felt for a damned long time. As if the press of her body to his was like touching an electric fence, Hayes dropped his hands immediately, broke off the kiss, and stepped back.

At least he didn't try to avoid looking at her.

Breathless, she stared back at him, cataloging his hooded eyes. The flush in his cheeks. His lips, still wet from her mouth. The erection testing the fly of his jeans.

"What was that?" she finally whispered. "What the fuck was that, Kelley?"

He huffed a deep, ragged breath, and lifted his hand. She winced, assuming he was going to swipe his hand over his mouth. To brush her away. Instead, he pinched the bridge of his nose and shook his head.

Eyes closed, he answered, "Just wanted to make you stop talking."

Not sure that was any better than if he had wiped her kiss

off his lips, Jessica simply stared at him. Anger and hurt warred in her belly. She wasn't angry that he had kissed her. She was angry that she wanted more. Still. Even after he confessed to kissing her only to shut her up, she wanted more.

"Maybe next time tell me to stop talking," she suggested.

Hayes nodded and stepped up to the sink. "I'll finish this here."

Jessica untied the apron, slipped it off, and tossed it on the counter.

"Yeah. I'll be back later."

She stormed out of the kitchen, but rather than heading to the back entrance, she went to the dining room to grab her coat and purse. On knees that trembled with shock or worse—desire—she stuffed her hands in her pockets and walked the three blocks home. She had exactly two hours to get her head on straight, to get her heartrate back to normal, and change clothes for work. Where she would have to see Hayes Kelley all night.

That made her furious. Having to look at him all night and make his flippant comment about kissing her to shut her up jive with the erection she'd felt pressed to her middle.

DESPITE HER ANGER, her nerves, Jessica reported to work at the regular time and marched inside like nothing crazy had happened in the kitchen hours earlier. She barely glanced at the kitchen as she stepped into her office and put her purse on her desk.

"Gonna be a great night!"

She looked up with a frown that might scare some people, but when she saw Capri's big smile, Jessica felt her anger soften.

"We're like two weeks out from Christmas!" Capri squealed. "I think we're booked almost solid from now 'til Christmas Eve."

"Good!" Jessica nodded. She meant it. The restaurant's good fortune was her good fortune. And she loved the Chop House, the people here. Maybe not *Hayes Kelley, rude kisser.* But most of the people here were her friends.

"Hayes wants us all up front in five for a pep talk," Capri told her.

Jessica shrugged out of her coat and rolled her eyes, back to Capri.

"'kay. Be right there."

Hayes probably wanted to rip everyone a new butthole after the incident in the kitchen. And Jessica figured he would make it her fault. Like she had thrown herself at him and locked her lips on his. Like she had been the one to slide her tongue into his mouth and grab him by the hips and reel him in.

No. No, she knew Hayes. He would say it was her fault because she talked too much. *Jerk.* She thought they were friends. So when she saw the way he interacted with the kids today, she had been genuinely curious. And she had asked a question. A simple question that had nothing to do with him needing to put his mouth anywhere near hers to answer her.

Jessica hung her coat up, locked her purse in the bottom desk drawer, and headed to the front wishing she could hit the bourbon before they opened. She had worn her favorite outfit tonight, not to entice Hayes. But because she loved it, and the beige-colored wide legged trousers and shimmery brown blouse made her feel like a queen.

Take that, Hayes Kelley.

The heeled boots were icing on the cake, like a crown for a queen. They made her tall enough to look him right in the eyes, she realized too late. Hayes stood at the bar with the rest of the employees gathered around him. He flicked his gaze over her briefly and continued on with his glowering, mean, threatening look.

"What's up, Hayes?" Hampton leaned forward to rest his elbows on the bar.

Hayes tapped an envelope on the bar, an envelope Jessica hadn't realized he was holding. Had one of their customers written in to complain about their food or service? Jessica had seldom seen Hayes get mad. She had seen him correct his employees, though never in a condescending way. But she hadn't seen him fire anyone.

"Um." Hayes scratched the back of his head and looked at the envelopes in his hand again. *Envelopes? Yep.* Jessica couldn't tell how many, but there was more than one. "It's the holidays, and um, maybe you guys need some cash for shopping. Or maybe you'd like to treat yourself. I just wanted to say thank you, again. A restaurant is only as good as its reputation, and we're only as good as the people around us. The Chop House is, in my humble opinion, the best restaurant in Holly Creek. And so that means, we must all work pretty well together."

He glanced at Jessica and held the stare for a moment. She simply stared back, unwilling to blink or look away.

"Anyway. I appreciate all of you. The time and work you put in. Merry Christmas." He looked at the envelope on top and handed it to Capri. The next he studied and gave to Hampton. Their names were on the envelopes. Which could mean differing amounts as bonuses or holiday gifts. Personal notes or gifts.

Jessica wondered if hers would be a membership for the mouthwash of the month club or a handwritten apology. Didn't matter. She'd shred either. Hers, of course, was the last in his hand. Everyone else had dispersed, gone back to their working stations, by that time. But still, Hayes simply handed her the envelope, as he unapologetically looked her up and down.

She snatched it from him with a muttered thanks and turned to head back to her office. Without opening the envelope, she tossed it on her desk, and headed back up front to greet this evening's diners.

CHAPTER 24

*H*ayes

When his ounce pour of bourbon was gone, and Jessica hadn't joined him outside, Hayes assumed she had slipped out the front to avoid him and gone home. He didn't blame her for being pissed off, but he couldn't apologize if she didn't let him talk, could he?

The hell of it was that kiss had fried his brain and his dick. He hadn't planned to do it; well, he had thought about it a time or two in the past couple of weeks. But not in any serious way. Nope, she had been talking, and without knowing it, her questions and suggestions on him having a family had been like a little kid digging and digging in a pile of rocks. Deeper and deeper. Making a bigger mess.

He had kissed her to shut her up.

The first time.

And then he had kissed her again because she smelled good, and her eyes had sparkled like snowflakes in sunlight when they were out on the sledding hill, and because he liked her.

Which told him how fucked up he was. And how badly he had fucked up the situation. All he was supposed to do was drive her to the city on the twenty-second of December, put on a stupid monkey suit, and be her date. Which would include dining with a bunch of rich people he would never have to see again, probably a dance or two with her—which he'd done and survived once—and then not sleep in the same bed as she did the night of the wedding. Bring her home. End of story.

And he had blown that ship right out of the damned water.

They had been busy tonight. Booked solid for reservations. His sous chefs had worked their asses off, the waitresses had been incredible—busy, but always smiling and friendly. Sure, it was probably partly due to the little bonus he had handed out before they opened. But more than that, it was the holiday season. People in Holly Creek loved the holidays. Even Jessica had been all smiles and small talk tonight. With everyone but him, anyway.

Was she pissed because he kissed her? Because he might be out of the game as far as dating went, but that little sound she had made in her throat—that was her admission that she was as turned on by the kiss as he was. Times might change, but certain things didn't. Physical attraction and lust didn't change because societal rules did.

Maybe she was pissed because he hadn't asked her first.

Then again, if he had put his finger over her lips to shush her and asked if he could kiss her, she might have slapped him stupid.

Tired of worrying about it, Hayes went back inside. The place was empty, save for Hampton and a few patrons at the bar.

"Headin' out?" Hampton called.

"I am." He nodded. The dinner rush was long gone; the

kitchen was closed. But it was possible Hampton would have more guests come in for a drink. "Holler if you need anything."

"Will do." Hampton nodded.

Hayes said a goodnight to the people at the bar, went to his office to grab his own coat, and left via the back door. He stopped to lock it behind him and then headed away on foot. His house was close enough to walk to and from the restaurant. But when he found himself at the corner where he needed to go left to his house, he hesitated a second and went right instead.

This close to midnight, it was quiet. In less than two weeks, he would be at the wedding with Jessica, and the city would be lit up and bustling, even at this hour. He dreaded the thought. He didn't mind the idea of being with Jessica a bit, but damned if he wanted to share her with all of New York City.

The side streets had been cleared of snow, but the yards off the beaten path looked more pristine. None of the slushy gray snow from traffic thrown up on the curbs and easements. In the streetlights, he saw a few snowmen that brought to mind snow days of his past.

Some of the houses he passed were dark, while others were lit with Christmas lights. He was cold, but the weather didn't bother him until the temperatures dropped below zero. After a crazy night at the Chop House, he liked the crisp, cold air on his face. Needed it tonight, especially, after what had happened in his kitchen earlier.

Her house was lit up. Not just the outdoor lights. But through her front window, Hayes could see her Christmas tree. Lamplight crossed her snowy yard, like a beacon showing him to her porch. The low murmur of a TV broke the silence as he stood at the front door ready to knock.

Was he ready? Hell, he had no idea what to even say to her.

And yet, if he didn't do something now, the little fuck up in his kitchen earlier would grow into something bigger, and maybe unfixable. Kind of like earlier at the Chop House, his fist was pounding on the door before he knew he was going to move.

He winced at the way the noise carried down the quiet little street. What if she was sleeping? What if she wasn't alone? But who would she be with? If she had a boyfriend, she wouldn't need Hayes as a wedding date, would she?

The door opened suddenly, and there she was. Tonight, her pajama pants looked like red silk with a snowflake print. She wore an oversized white t-shirt on top and nothing else. In the tree light, through the storm door, Hayes could see the outline of her nipples.

He should have called first.

But she would have let him go to voicemail.

Jessica stared at him for a moment and finally reached to push the door open and let him in.

"What do you want?" She crossed her arm over her chest, blocking his view of her breasts. Probably for the best, but damned if he didn't want to look one more time before she kicked him out.

He sighed and pushed the door closed behind him.

"I'm sorry."

Jessica stared at him for a long, silent moment. Finally, she turned her back to him and padded barefoot back to the sofa. Hayes watched her and noticed the tree for the first time. She had done it all in the gold, crème, and brown she had considered. It looked elegant and still warm and inviting.

Her TV was paused on a scene from *It's a Wonderful Life*. He knew the movie inside out, because he and his mom watched it together every year when he was a kid.

"What're you sorry for, Hayes?" She sat on the sofa, knees

drawn up under her, and pulled a fleece blanket over her lap. Her sharp gaze stole his breath away.

"This is a test, isn't it?"

She didn't laugh. Instead, she simply shrugged a shoulder and waited for him to speak.

He wasn't sorry for kissing her. Even if that was what she was angry about, he couldn't apologize for that. And he wouldn't take it back or change it, even if he could. No, what he was sorry for was bound to get him another night or two in the doghouse, but maybe he would get points for honesty.

If not, at least he would know where he stood with this bizarre need he couldn't shake.

"I'm sorry that today's the first time I kissed you," he said quietly. If he had expected her to throw something at him, he would be disappointed. His words had surprised her. She tipped her head and watched him expectantly. "I'm sorry that I've worked with you all these years and never noticed how pretty you are. Never said so."

She licked her lips and dipped her chin to her chest.

"I'm sorry that I quit kissing you when I did, and I'm sorry that I told you I kissed you to shut you up."

"Why did you kiss me, then?" she asked, eyes on her hands, folded in her lap.

"Well, because I've been thinking about it for a long time now, and because you were talking about me having kids, and obviously, I'm *not* gonna have kids. Because I'm never gonna find a woman to stick here in Holly Creek with a guy who tolerates Christmas at best and doesn't believe in marriage and forever, and you kept talking, and even though, I'm not lonely without a woman—" He hesitated when she threw the blanket off but continued. "Yes, Bradshaw. Yes, I very much wanted kids, and I needed to shut you up, so I kissed—"

CHAPTER 25

*J*essica

She wouldn't throw herself at him. Because what if he stepped away? Again? Instead, Jessica mimicked his moves from earlier that afternoon. She cupped his face in her hands, thrilling at the rasp of his scruff on her fingers and her palms. His eyes were wide as she stood on her tiptoes and pulled his face down to kiss him.

He smelled like bourbon. What would he taste like? As much as she wanted to know, she wouldn't hurry. She played at his lips, brushing hers over his again and again, loving the feel of that soft, scruffy beard on her mouth, her chin. When he sighed, when he linked his arms around her back, she breathed deeply, ruined now for bourbon any other way than on his breath, his lips.

Hungry for more of him, Jessica kissed a trail from his lips to his neck and nipped at a spot just under his ear. She wanted all of him, to devour him but to savor him at the same time. Hayes groaned quietly when she flicked his ear with the tip of her tongue.

"Bradshaw." He ground her name out like a prayer, desperately, pleadingly. His need drew her back, her lips on his as much for her as for him. Ready to taste him, she licked his lips and stroked her tongue inside his mouth.

The answering stroke of his over hers scorched a trail from her mouth to her core. Whatever the hell this was, she wanted more. Greedy, impatient, she dropped her hands to the front of his coat and yanked at the zipper. Hayes took mercy on her and pulled the zipper free to shrug out of his coat.

"Are you sure?" His gruff voice chased a shudder through her, a tiny hint of what other things his mouth might do.

"Yes."

Ready now to launch herself at him, to rip open his shirt and mold her hands over his hard chest—she had been thinking about it since the morning they danced, and she rested her head on him when she laughed—she whimpered softly as his hands found her instead.

Cold and rough on her warm belly. Smoothing over her hips, up her back, and finally around to cup her breasts.

"Ohmygod." She dropped her head back and moaned. Eyes locked on his, she watched him watch himself thumb her nipples, her thin shirt still covering her, his hands.

"So fucking beautiful." His voice broke, like he pushed the words out over broken glass.

"Hayes." Her word was a plea, everything she wanted and couldn't concentrate to ask for. She sighed with relief when he ducked his head, but he only closed his lips around the material still covering her nipple. "Please."

He drew back to look her in the eyes.

"The only condoms I have have been in my wallet for at least a year, if not two."

"I'll take the chance," she whispered.

"As much as I want you, I might tear right through them."

She nodded. "Me, too. Please, Hayes."

He skimmed his fingers down her belly and gathered her shirt in his hands. Her house was warm, but chills puckered her skin when he pulled the shirt over her head and tossed it aside.

"Fuck." He clenched his teeth, his wide eyes taking in her nakedness. Jessica lifted his chin and looked him in the eyes. She nodded her head toward her bedroom and took his hand. Hayes followed her to the open door, but when she stopped there, he reached around her, stroked his hands up her belly, and cupped her breasts again.

"I want everything you can give me," she whispered as she dropped her head back to rest on his chest. "I want it all right now."

She turned in his arms and reached for his shirt.

"You're gonna have to let me lead here, Jess." He caught her hand and drew it to his mouth to kiss her fingers. "I haven't been with a woman in a long time. You touch me in the right place, and I'm gonna blow my wad like a fuckin' fountain before we get started."

Stunned by his admission, she swallowed hard and nodded.

"Okay." She licked her lips. "Take charge, Hayes. I'm yours."

He gritted his teeth and tugged her hand down to cover his fly. His cock was hard as steel under her palm. Jessica stepped backwards, toward her bed. Hayes shrugged out of his shirt and then shucked his t-shirt, too. Both fell to the floor, immediately forgotten.

Jessica admired the view. His hard biceps and wide shoulders. A few sparse hairs covered his well-defined chest. Her eyes trailed lower to the dark hair just above his jeans. Her knees shook as he pulled his wallet from his pocket and found the condoms inside it.

Slipping her fingers inside her pajama pants, under the lace of her panties, she pushed both down slowly and shimmied out of them.

"You." Hayes groaned his approval. "You are so beautiful."

"Make me feel beautiful," she whispered.

Like her words flipped a switch, Hayes was on her. Gentle but strong hands cupped her butt and lifted her to press her bare breasts to his chest. Not sure if the sigh of pleasure was hers or his, she dug her fingers into his hair and met his lips when he kissed her.

He eased her backward to lie on her bed, trailed sweet, hot kisses over her chest and belly, and then worshipped her on his knees at the foot of her bed. Jessica writhed under him, her head tipped up to watch him kiss her, until she lost control and fell back to the bed, the delicious orgasm tearing through her like a runaway train. Even when her body quivered under his lips, his tongue, he kissed her. His hands smoothing her thighs, her belly, stroking her core until she exploded again, white heat racing through her veins, her body tingling with pleasure.

"I think I like you better than bourbon."

Still panting, she met his eyes as he stood at the end of her bed and kicked his jeans and underwear off. The cocky grin on his face made her want to come again. She slipped her fingers between her legs as he opened the condom and rolled it on.

"What're you—?" He cut himself off, eyes locked on her fingers sliding over her core, still wet from his mouth, from her pleasure.

"Smile at me again."

"Smile?" He laughed.

"Yep. Cocky, like you knew you could get me off."

"I did know." He crawled up the bed and settled over her

spread legs to watch her play. Jessica moved slowly, eyes roaming from his to her fingers to his cock, thick and hard for her. He peeked up at her and grinned when he caught her looking. "Because I would grovel at your feet for hours if that's what it took to make you come like that, Bradshaw."

She panted softly and laughed when he quirked his eyebrow at her.

"The next time you look at me like that at work, I'm gonna explode."

"Just don't do this in your office." He lowered his eyes to her fingers again. "Or we might have a problem."

Jessica closed her eyes for a moment, feeling him move over her. His lips closed around her nipple and tugged. That same wave of heat washed over her sending her over the edge. She yelled his name as she let her hand fall to the bed, limp beside her.

Hayes slid his hand under her thigh, stroked it up to cup her butt cheek, and drove into her in one smooth, deep stroke. Greedy and ready for him yet again, she looped her arms around his shoulders to hang on as she moved her hips to meet him stroke for stroke.

CHAPTER 26

*H*ayes

She was tight and hot around his cock, her arms around his shoulders loose. She combed her fingers through his hair and dragged them down his neck, only to sink her nails into his shoulders. He wasn't sure, but he might have moaned or mewled or made some noise of satisfaction. Jessica moved beneath him, arching her back, meeting him thrust for thrust. Hayes devoured every inch of her his mouth, his teeth, could reach. Her parted lips as she kissed him back. Her neck. The hollow at the base of her throat. Collarbones. The pale, curves of her breasts. The flick of his tongue over her nipple drew a long, thick moan from her parted lips. Hayes tipped his head up to peek at her. Head thrown back, eyes closed, and her teeth now digging into her own lip, she was the picture of a woman enjoying her body.

And his body.

When he shifted slightly over her, she sighed in protest and smoothed her hands over his back. She drove her hips up from the bed to meet him, harder, faster, and dug her fingers into his ass to pull him deeper.

Hayes hadn't been this fucking deep inside a woman in so long. How the hell he had lasted the past several years without this insanely, incredible feeling—the wet slide of her walls around him, the way she squeezed him inside her body, her hands sculpting his arms and back. How the hell had he worked with her for ten years and not known how hot it would be to take her to bed?

Jessica fitted the soles of her feet over his calf muscles and smoothed them down his legs. Ridiculous that such a simple action could ramp up his need, his desperation, to shatter her, but it did. Hayes pulled out of her completely and drove hard and deep again. She locked her ankles around his waist and cut loose with a deep, delicious groan. When he peeked at her this time, she was smiling, panting, eyes closed.

"God, I love this," she whispered. "You feel so fucking good inside me. Keep riding."

"Are you okay?"

She blinked at him and laughed softly. "Keep riding, Kelley. Seems I haven't blown your mind just yet."

"You blew my mind when you answered the door in your pajamas. All the fucking decorations in the world, and all I wanted to look at was your nipples outlined in that shirt."

"Don't hold back," she whispered.

Maybe it was what she said, maybe it was the throaty whisper. Maybe it was the way she tightened her walls around his cock again. And maybe it was her fingertips smoothing over his face, into his hair, and the flick of her tongue around her lips. Hayes dipped his head for a kiss and pumped into her harder and faster again and again, until that wall of heat exploded inside him, around him. The world could burn down around them for all he cared. Hayes collapsed on her, rested his forehead on her shoulder, and struggled to breathe as his body burned with aftershocks.

Neither of them moved or spoke for several long moments. Hayes finally slid off her to lay at her side with his head on her chest. Her steady heartbeat pounded in his ear.

"How did we never do this before?" she mumbled with a small laugh.

"I can honestly say I never considered touching this way until recently."

"So, it's Chelsea's fault."

He lifted his head to look her in the eyes.

"No. I think it was me. When Lisa left me, I was...kind of dead inside. And after trying to move on—"

"Hooking up?" she corrected him with a quirked eyebrow.

"A time or two," he admitted, "I gave up. Decided it wasn't for me. You were a kid—"

"Jesus, Hayes, I'm not a kid." She rolled her eyes.

"You were, though. For a long time, you were a kid. And then when you weren't a kid anymore, you were a professional. And you run my restaurant better than I would. It never crossed my mind that..."

"That what?"

"That sex with Bradshaw would be so damned hot."

She grinned. "Look. I know this isn't..."

Hayes moved when she pushed herself up to rest on her elbows.

"I know you're not into relationships." She shrugged and met his eyes for a moment. "But would you just stay? Tonight?"

Hayes cupped her chin in his hand and brushed a kiss over her lips.

"You stay here. I'll go lock up and turn your TV off."

He slid over her legs to get to the side of the bed, but she stopped him with another kiss. Hayes tweaked her nipple as he climbed out of bed. She laughed and dropped back to lie down, eyes on him as he left her bedroom. Naked, he strode down the short hall to the living room and locked her door. He found the TV remote on the sofa, under the fleece blanket she had used to hide herself from him earlier.

TV off, the only lights in the house were the white lights of the tree. He stood for a moment and admired it. No question Jessica Bradshaw was too good for him. He would never be good enough to deserve a woman like her. Best to remind himself of that.

He would climb back into her bed tonight and spend the next several hours giving her every ounce of pleasure he could. And then he would go with her to Chelsea Calhoun's wedding. And then they would go back to business as usual—Hayes, a good-ole-boy stuck in a small town with a rusted old pickup and an addiction to holding a cigarette because he was too much of a pussy to snap it and walk away or light it and suck down the poison and Jessica, a beautiful young woman with stars in her eyes and the world in her hands.

"Mmm." She sighed when he climbed back into bed beside her. "Missed you."

"I was looking at your tree," he told her.

"Yeah? What do you think?"

"Do you want me to be honest?"

She roared with laughter and climbed over to straddle him. "I don't want you to talk at all."

"Where's the other condom?"

Her laughter filled the dark room as she inched back over his legs.

"You don't have to do that, Bradshaw—"

"I want my mouth on you," she said simply.

CHAPTER 27

*J*essica

A full week after sleeping with Hayes Kelley, Jessica was still feeling it. The euphoria. The lightheartedness. Happiness. Thankfully, the holidays were just around the corner, so no one would suspect the reason her smile might be a bit bigger and brighter had anything to do with the way Hayes had worked her over. And he had worked her over. When she closed her eyes at night, she could still feel the weight of his body over hers. The heat of his skin sliding over hers as they moved together.

They hadn't talked about it. The morning after hadn't been awkward; in fact, Jessica thought it was perfectly warm and cozy. Hayes, back to his grumpy self, had insisted he make the coffee because hers was too weak. She had only laughed at him. Made breakfast. They sat at her table, him in his jeans and t-shirt and her in his flannel, buttoned over her nudity, and talked about the Chop House. Jessica loved to get under his skin just by suggesting different names for his place, names that fit in with the holiday theme in Holly Creek. It was so easy to rile him; she was like a tiny splinter wedging itself in his finger and making him crazy.

She couldn't wait for the wedding now. How yummy was he going to be in a tuxedo? His hazel eyes. Little bit of five o'clock shadow on his face. Her knees went weak any time she thought about that scruff on his face, the way it felt on her belly and her thighs.

"Look." Amelia sighed. "It's Blue Crawford."

Jessica looked up to see Blue step inside the high school gym. She liked the guy well enough, but she didn't know him too well. He kept to himself, so most people—even those born and raised in Holly Creek—didn't know him too well.

"I think every soul in Holly Creek has been in here today," Amelia said with a frown. She stood on her tiptoes and surveyed the crowd.

"They usually are," Jessica reminded her. The Holly Creek Cookie Walk was one of the biggest community holiday events. Their mom loved to bake, so each year, she made all kinds of cookies and volunteered to work and dragged Jessica and Amelia with her. Not that they minded. It was always a fun day —by then, the whole town was decorated and hyped for Christmas, everyone dropped in for cookies at some point in the day, so they visited with friends and neighbors, and the cookies were delicious.

"I think your Scrooge cookies are outdoing last year's gingerbread men," Amelia told their mom.

"I don't like gingerbread." Jessica turned her nose up.

"They're fun to make, though." Mom smiled and stepped aside to talk to the woman at the table next to them.

"You look like you've been eating special cookies," Amelia told Jessica.

"What does that mean?" Jessica asked. She shook her head,

ready to deny whatever Amelia was about to say. Like an accusation that she'd slept with Hayes.

"Weed." Amelia shrugged.

Jessica snorted. "You think I'm smoking dope?"

"No, but you look like it." Amelia blasted a big smile at Dr. Addison and his wife and kids.

"Mommy!" Their youngest pointed at the plate of Scrooge cookies. Jessica fought her need to explain that the cookies weren't moldy, that there was green food coloring in them. "Those cookies are the Scrooge!"

Amelia laughed and chatted Lila up as she and her youngest picked out cookies to add to their box.

"Merry Christmas!" Lila said as they all moved on.

"What I really think," Amelia said out of the side of her mouth, "is that at some point, Hayes Kelley banged the hell out of you, and you're still on cloud nine."

Jessica pressed her lips together, willing her body not to heat up, her cheeks to flush with embarrassment.

"How was it?" Amelia asked her.

A laugh rumbled up from her belly and slipped out.

"Pretty incredible," she answered simply.

"Seriously?!" Amelia turned to her with a squeal.

"Ssh." Jessica did blush that time. "We're keeping it quiet."

"Why?"

"Why wouldn't we?" she asked with a shrug. "It was just sex."

"Right." Amelia rolled her eyes. "The guy is sex on a stick. He's fun. He owns a successful restaurant. And he's hot for you."

"It was just sex."

"You can say that to anyone else and make them believe it, Jess," Amelia argued. "But I know you. You're in love with him."

"I don't have to be in love with anyone just because I slept with him."

"No. You don't." Amelia nodded. Jessica flinched at the look of concern on her sister's face. "But you've been in love with him since you came back from college."

"Whatever."

"You're blind, Sis. You guys have been like an old, married couple the entire time you've worked for him as his manager. I'm just glad you finally consummated that work marriage. You deserve a little love."

Jessica swallowed hard and looked away. Amelia was right. Jessica had thought she was being childish, silly. Thinking she loved him just because they slept together. Just because the sex had been so hot. Hayes wasn't interested in her turning into a goofy, girly ditz who saw stars and talked about love and marriage. She was determined to push through the post-sex crush and get things back to normal.

But Amelia's words rang true.

She loved working with Hayes. She knew how to shovel his shit, his grumpiness. She knew how to make him laugh, even when he tried so hard not to. And she loved how he talked about his mom, the way he still spent time with his dad.

"Yeah." Jessica nodded and shrugged. "Well. Sounds nice, but that's not what it was. We just blew off a little steam."

"Hmm." Amelia licked her lips and nodded. "Speak of the devil."

Jessica turned to see Hayes step around from behind her. Had he heard them talking? The tables were arranged side by side, four rows deep. Some people walked the tables in order to see the cookies on display, and some people twisted in and out of the rows to greet people they knew. Hayes could have been doing either of those things. And he could have heard every word she and Amelia just exchanged.

"Hey." She flashed him a grin, hoping it was casual. Nonchalant.

She had known the night they were together that it would be a one-time thing. And still, it had hurt a little to watch him walk out of her house the next morning after breakfast. No more kisses. No handholding. Just a thank you for breakfast and see ya later.

"Bradshaw." He nodded, his lips in a tight grin.

"Get any cookies yet?"

He nodded as he surveyed their mom's table.

"Yeah. I think I've eaten a dozen so far."

He jerked his gaze up at her when she snorted.

"I'm not kidding." He thumped his belly—hard and firm, she remembered. She had slid over him and licked a trail from his neck to his—"I need an antacid."

"Try a mint cookie," Amelia suggested.

He aimed a smile in her direction. "Your guy just pulled into the parking lot when I passed the window at the far end of the gym."

"Nice."

Jessica winced at the flash of envy at the way Amelia's face lit up.

"It's not official yet," Amelia said, "but we've been talking about a nice place for weddings."

Hayes cringed. "Not you, too, Bruce."

Jessica snorted. "A bit of a misquote, but I see what you're goin' for there."

He laughed, but his eyes were sad.

"Don't say New York," Jessica glanced at Amelia.

"No. We were thinking either a big wedding here or a destination wedding. On a beach somewhere."

"Don't waste your money, kid," Hayes told her. He shook his head. "If you defy the odds and stay married, you can put money toward a house payment or a kid or something."

"And he's back." Jessica tipped her head and narrowed her eyes at him. "I put my dress and heels on and did the whole shebang." She waved her hand at her face and hair. "I'm good to go. You?"

"You didn't say I'd have to wear heels," he grumbled.

Jessica read the way he stepped back from the table. Jammed his hands in his pockets. They had spent the week together, working, same as always. No sneaking off to the offices to play around. No quick kisses. No looks of longing. Just the same as always.

And now he was making it clear he regretted the things they had done together.

"Does your tux fit?" She raised her brows at him, irritated. Hurt. Angry at herself for falling for him, for not being able to sleep with him and walk away no strings attached. And embarrassed for her sister to see the aftermath of that incredibly hot sex.

"It won't if I keep eating cookies," he mumbled.

"Then quit. Get out of here."

His lips twitched up in a half grin, but she could still see the sadness in his eyes.

CHAPTER 28

*H*ayes

He didn't hear every word they said. But he didn't need to. They were sisters; they were talking. Animatedly, and then, Amelia got that look on her face. They were talking about the night he and Jessica spent together. It wasn't that he didn't want anyone to know; he'd pay for a billboard ad or put it in neon. But Jessica deserved more than what he could give her, and in a town like Holly Creek, people got nosey and pushy. It was in Jessica's best interest to keep what happened between them quiet.

The line about the cookies hadn't been a lie. He had eaten way too damned many. And though he hadn't been on a drinking binge by any means, he had guzzled a few beers between that night with Jessica and today at the cookie walk. He'd hit the bourbon a bit harder. Enough that he felt like shit. His stomach was bothering him when he came into work earlier.

Then again, that could all be a line of bullshit he was

feeding himself. He was nervous. Uncomfortable. About seeing Jessica. The whole last week with her had been fine because she hadn't acted different around him after they had sex. Even that next morning, she had kept things casual. She had laughed at him, rolled her eyes at him, when he complained about her weak coffee. She made breakfast. Sure, she did it wearing his damned shirt, and fuck, if she didn't look like a pretty little dessert parading around with the tail of that flannel barely covering her cute little ass. But she hadn't come onto him. She hadn't asked for more. She hadn't demanded kisses or promises.

She got it.

Except she didn't. Not if she was sharing details with her sister.

She had appeared normal earlier when she came in. Dressed in black slacks and a shimmery red blouse, she was the same professional Jessica she had been before he had parted her legs and tasted her. She talked to him through the evening, calling out times on tables, requesting special options for particular diners, conveying kudos and thank yous to him from their patrons. Just the same as always. And yet, there was something in her eyes when she didn't think he was looking. Not hopeful, not like she believed they could be more.

But sad.

Like she knew they couldn't ever be more than that one night.

When the kitchen closed, and the stainless steel shined like diamonds, he found her at the bar with Hampton and Capri. Blue Crawford, of all people, was seated at the far end of the bar talking to Hampton.

Jessica looked up and met his eyes. He splashed a bit of bourbon in a glass and nodded to the back, as if he needed to tell her where he was going. Maybe he was inviting her to join him. Maybe this thing, this worry, was all his imagination. Hell, maybe Jessica had told Amelia but maybe she had only been into the physical things—maybe right now Amelia Bradshaw had a pretty good idea how big or small his dick was, whatever information Jessica had fed her.

But he doubted it. She wasn't a prude. But she wasn't the kind of woman to share those details lightly.

He grabbed his Carhartt off the hook in his office and headed outside. The door closed and killed the jazzy Christmas music in the Chop House. But it was seven days before Christmas in Holly Creek, so of course, classic Christmas carols played from speakers all up and down Main Street. His place included.

Right now, Hayes wanted to tell Burl Ives to jump off the bridge and take his holly jolly Christmas with him. Every night this week, when she had come outside to sit with him, she had sung along to every damned carol that played. Off-key. Corny. Happy.

She didn't need Hayes around to bring her down. To take away that happy.

The door opened behind him. Closed. Her heels clicked on the asphalt as she made her way to the table to sit down. Not singing, but humming tonight. He looked at her as she sat beside him. Tonight, instead of bourbon, she held a coffee mug.

"You won't sleep." He frowned at her.

"I'm cold. It's got Bailey's in it."

"Mm." He nodded.

They sat quietly for a while. Hayes wasn't sure if she felt the tension, or if it was just him. If guilt for using her was clawing away inside him. Digging into his chest, his throat, making it hard to breathe.

"Look."

"Don't."

From the corner of his eye, he saw her shake her head.

"It's not love, Bradshaw." He cleared his throat. "I like you. We work well together. But."

"I don't remember asking you to love me."

He might have believed her if her voice wasn't thick with emotion.

"I don't love anyone. Maybe I did my mom. I take care of my dad. But I got nothin'. Nothing to offer you."

"Can I ask you something?" She looked his way.

Hayes flinched, but he nodded.

"Why now? Why after a week of things being totally cool between us are you doing this now?"

He sighed and shrugged dramatically. "I dunno. I just don't want you to get any ideas."

"Fuck you, Kelley." She rolled her eyes. "What a bullshit jerk thing to say to me after all we've been through together."

"What?"

"What? You think you gave me this night of smokin' hot sex? Like your dick is all that? And now you have to remind the little lady it didn't mean anything?"

"Bradshaw—"

"I didn't ask you for a thing," she snapped. "I didn't ask you for promises. I didn't ask you to fucking kiss me goodbye. So why, now, do you think I'm gonna beg you for something?'

"What did you say to Amelia?"

"Seriously?" She narrowed her eyes at him. "Did you hear us?"

"Not really. But you're sisters. And you were in this deep conversation—"

"And so, naturally, we had to be talking about how good you are in bed?"

"Jesus." He groaned and threw back the last of the bourbon in his glass.

"You're a dick," she announced as she eased back off the table to stand in front of him. "I have never asked you for anything—"

"You asked me to stay," he reminded her.

"I did." She flinched. "Because I knew that night was it. And I wanted more. Sex. Nothing else."

He dipped his head and scrubbed his fingers up through the back of his hair, knocking his hat to the ground.

"But you know what, Hayes?"

"What?" He blew out a deep breath, angry with himself, with her, with the situation. Wishing it was over. Wishing it had never happened.

Wishing it could end differently. Somehow.

"Even if I did love you," she shrugged, "it's not your concern."

"What does that mean?"

"You fucked me. You sign my paychecks." She stared at him boldly. "But you don't get to know what's going on in my head or my heart. Ever."

"I don't want you to love me, Bradshaw. It won't get you anywhere—"

"I'm off the clock," she said softly. "And you can't tell me what to do."

He flinched when she swung her cup to the side, tossing the coffee and Irish crème out on the ground. She stalked around him without another word.

"What about the wedding?" he asked as she pulled the door open.

"I'd rather deal with Rex's groomsmen than with a chauvinistic jackass like you."

The door banged closed.

Gene Autry was signing about Rudolph.

Hayes Kelley clenched his teeth so hard he thought his head would break.

CHAPTER 29

*J*essica

Avoiding Hayes at work was easy enough. For one thing, the place was hopping. Holiday shoppers having a fancy dinner before going home for the evening. Families in town for holiday visits enjoyed dinner at Kelley's Chop House. Jessica marveled at the number of couples just out for romantic dinners in the week before Christmas.

She eyed a young couple from the hostess' stand, wishing she and Amelia hadn't had that little sisterly talk at the cookie walk. Maybe if Amelia had kept her thoughts to herself, Jessica wouldn't have realized she had feelings for Hayes. And this whole situation could have just worked itself out naturally. Instead, Jessica felt like a stupid kid with a crush on her boss. A boss who happened to be anti-love, anti-relationship, anti-Christmas, anti-anything fun or emotional in the world.

The door opened drawing her attention away from the couple and their bottle of wine. Just as well that Hayes had shut her down the other night before she said anything stupid.

She would never have this kind of night with someone like Hayes. He would never take her out for a nice dinner—not just because he worked six nights a week. But fine dining, wine, candlelight wasn't his style.

She liked wine. And romantic candle lit dinners. And guys who didn't act like it pained them to smile. She was simply confusing good sex with an emotional connection.

The music outside—Darlene Love's version of "Christmas" —drowned out the jazzy instrumental "Jingle Bells" currently playing softly inside the Chop House. Wilson Kelley stepped inside. Dressed in nice flat-front khakis and a blue button-down shirt under a leather coat, he looked like an older, dressier, handsome version of the jerk in the kitchen. Jessica moved to greet them, taking in the other gentleman and two women with them. Wilson Kelley had a dinner date. She wondered if Hayes had known he was coming in tonight.

She heard the other man give his name to Afton. So, the reservations hadn't been under Wilson's name. *Interesting.*

"Hello." She stepped closer to the group and offered them a warm smile. "Welcome to Kelley's Chop House."

She could count the number of times she had seen Wilson inside this place on one hand. And one of those two times, he had come in just before they opened to borrow Hayes' truck keys.

"You're Bradshaw." Wilson quirked an eyebrow at her.

What the hell did that mean?

"Yes," she said with a smile, hoping it wasn't obvious that he had rattled her. "Jessica Bradshaw. How are you this evening, Mr. Kelley?"

"Wilson." He shook his head and waved the formal title away. "I'm well, thank you. These people insisted we have dinner here tonight instead of the bar."

Jessica laughed softly.

"Enjoy your dinner." She nodded at all of them as Afton led the foursome away to their table.

Hampton whistled quietly. "That's the boss man's dad, isn't it?"

"It is," Jessica said with a sincere smile. Good for him. She had no idea if the woman with him was his girlfriend, or if this was a first date for them. Or if they were just a group of friends out for a festive evening. But seeing Wilson Kelley dressed nicely, wearing that warm smile, made her happy. Maybe someday his grinch son would find something to make him happy.

As she had been doing since the night Hayes had dumped her even though she had never assumed they were a couple, she left through the front door. She missed the unwinding time with him out back. She missed him. Not just the feel of his hands on her body, but his grumpy face when she talked too much. The way part of his mouth smiled at something she said, even when it was obvious it pained him to do so. She missed the way they always talked out an evening, if something needed improvement. If their wait staff was efficient. If the bacon-wrapped scallops were overcooked.

But she had no interest in sitting beside him in the cold and not talking. Knowing that somehow her ridiculous crush was obvious, like some kind of beaming light shining from her heart or maybe big cartoon hearts in her eyes. Knowing that he regretted every second of the night they spent together because now she had turned into a clingy, insecure woman.

And she no interest in sitting next to him in the cold and talking. Pretending that nothing had changed. Maybe she would get there, but she needed some time. If he hadn't just announced out of the blue that he didn't love her, that the sex was just sex, she would be fine. She could pretend with the best of the actors on Broadway. But having been called out on it hurt. It embarrassed her.

Her phone buzzed the second she entered her house. It was possible it was Amelia calling, but she doubted it. Most likely Hayes. Maybe he was calling to tell her he had reconsidered and wanted the bonus money back that he had given her. Maybe he wanted to make sure she understood that their one night of burning up the sheets didn't entitle her to a Christmas gift.

She turned her phone off without looking at it. Stripped down and put her pajamas on. Not the ones she wore the night Hayes had shown up here and undressed her and taken her to bed. Nope. Ugly gray and white fleece plaid. With holes in them. She avoided the mirror as she washed her face and brushed her teeth.

Tomorrow she would have to drive to New York for the rehearsal and then the wedding the next day. As happy as she was for Chelsea and Rex, she dreaded the weekend. The wedding. The people she didn't know. Showing up alone and dealing with Miriam Buchanan. She sure as hell had no desire to be set up with any of the groomsmen. Nope. She'd just grit her teeth and get through it.

Without Hayes.

She hadn't been sure about his offer to go with her, not that first day he had told Amelia he was going to be her date. But she had gotten comfortable with the idea. Even before they had slept together, Jessica had found herself looking forward to the wedding. To seeing Hayes in a tuxedo. To dancing with him.

She had even been looking forward to the three-hour drive

with him. She had a playlist of crazy Christmas songs ready to blast, to make him squirm.

And now, she would be making that drive alone and walking into the Plaza Hotel alone and subjecting herself to Rex's family and friends. Her anxiety would be through the roof before she ever left her house tomorrow.

At least having Hayes with her would have made that part easier. Eased the anxiety. Made her comfortable. She had assumed that was their friendship, that she felt safe with Hayes because they had known each other for so long.

Maybe Amelia was right. Maybe she really had been in love with Hayes Kelley all these years. Maybe that's why she never watched the clock or counted the seconds to get away during time spent with him.

CHAPTER 30

Hayes

Seeing the little red Ford parked in front of Jessica's house turned his usual frown into a scowl. He wasn't here to grovel, exactly, but he would have to apologize. Hayes didn't say the words I'm sorry too often; he didn't appreciate the idea of an audience when he said them in a few minutes.

Jessica had been avoiding him all week, since that ugly scene out back. He didn't care the first night, but by the second day, he missed talking to her. She managed to convey whatever she needed to for business reasons, but she had given him a cold shoulder for anything else. While he understood her reaction, he hated how badly he'd fucked things up.

She might very well slam the door in his face, but he wasn't going to let her drive to the city for the wedding without him. Well, without a *date*. He was under no illusion that she would forgive him for being a dick and suddenly be excited to have him as her escort.

If he was lucky, she would at least sort of forgive him and let him drive to the city. And drag him around as her date.

Lucky?

Hayes flinched and gave himself a mental shake as he climbed out of the truck. He reached to the back of the cab and took his travel bag from the clothes hook. His tux fit; he had tried it on the night they fought.

He heard the music when he climbed up the porch steps. That damned Wham! Song that everyone and their stupid dog played on repeat every year from Halloween to New Year's. Hayes steeled himself for the worst, took a deep breath, and knocked on the storm door. He stood for several moments waiting, but she didn't answer the door. The music was loud enough the neighborhood could probably hear it, and Amelia was here, so odds were, Jessica didn't hear him knock.

He could run. Turn his ass around and get right back in his truck and go home. Let her deal with the wedding and Rex's mother and the whole damned bet. But he wouldn't. Hell, he didn't give a rat's ass about the bet. He liked charity donations, and whether there would be video circulating of Jessica doing the chicken dance or not, he wouldn't leave her to go to the wedding alone.

Because she would be nervous. Not about the wedding. Not like she would worry she would trip going down an aisle or step on her groomsman's foot when they were dancing. But because she wasn't comfortable with crowds, and she didn't like big cities. She called it social anxiety; he called it smart. He didn't love crowds or big cities, either. But he could handle it.

He knocked again and this time tried the doorknob. Unlocked, it turned easily, so he pushed the door open to step inside.

"What the hell?!"

Her yelp drew his attention as she was walking out of her bathroom in only a pair of jeans and a bra. A pink lace bra with tiny cups that did absolutely nothing but make her breasts look fantastic. She cleared her throat and covered herself, her hands over her breasts. Hayes was reminded of how soft her skin was, the texture of her nipples on his tongue.

"What're you even doing here?" she snapped.

"Hayes."

He dragged his gaze away from Jessica to find Amelia propped in Jessica's bedroom doorway. Arms folded over her chest, a cat-that-ate-the-canary smile on her face.

"Are you ready?" He looked back at Jessica.

"For what?"

"To go."

She snorted and rolled her eyes. "Go home."

"I told you I would go with you to the wedding," he reminded her.

"I wouldn't want to lean on you, Hayes." Her voice was cool and sarcastic. "I know you don't deal well when people need you."

"Bradshaw." He huffed out a harsh breath and set his travel bag on the sofa. They stood at opposite ends of the house and stared at each other.

"I'm gonna get out of your way," Amelia announced. She looked over her shoulder into Jessica's bedroom. Hayes' body was at war with itself. His dick was ready to rock 'n' roll, but his gut hurt. His chest ached a little bit. He had loved every second with Jessica Bradshaw, but he wasn't sure even that one night of hot sex was worth destroying their friendship over.

Amelia glanced at him but turned her back to him and moved closer to Jessica. They shared a mumbled conversation; this time, one he wished he could hear and couldn't. He looked away when the girls hugged, and then Amelia whirled around and headed toward the living room. Toward him.

"Be smart," she told him as she snatched her keys and coat

from the chair. He had no idea what that meant. She flashed him a grim smile as she slipped out the door, leaving him alone with Jessica. When he looked back for her, Jessica slipped into her bedroom.

"I wasn't sure what time you wanted to leave."

She didn't answer him. Again, he wondered if she didn't hear him, or if she was ignoring him. Hayes wiped his boots on the rug by her door and moseyed down the hall. The last time he'd been here, he had followed a half-naked Jessica to her room, invited. Now he walked the gallows.

What if she insisted she was going alone?

What if she never talked to him again?

He found her zipping up her own garment bag, got just a peek of dark red satin. Mouth dry, he struggled to swallow. Jessica would be beautiful in that gown. He had to see her in it. Furthermore, he didn't want anyone else's hands on her this weekend. People did stupid things at weddings; Jessica would be nervous so she might drink more.

The thought of her hooking up with someone at the wedding made him see a whole different sort of red.

"I don't need you to go with me, Hayes," she said quietly. "I'll be fine."

"What about the bet?"

"What about it?" She straightened and stared at him deadpan. When he did it, it felt acceptable. Maybe like he was bored and okay letting someone know. The look on her face was a dismissal.

"You'll lose."

"Oh well." She sighed and reached for the hanger on her bag.

"I'll get it." He moved away from the door to get her bag.

"I got it," she argued. Their fingers brushed. Hayes felt a rush of warmth. Nothing sexual. Just a sweet rush of affection, familiarity. Jessica snatched her hand back, away from him.

"I'll drive, but I'd rather take your car."

"Why?" Her sigh was heavy with irritation.

"Because your car is a bit nicer to drive into the city for this glitzy wedding. It wouldn't be too glamorous to show up in my old truck."

"Why are you here? Why are you insisting on going? You didn't want to from the word go."

She grabbed another bag from the floor by her bed and shoved past him on the way out of her room.

"Look, Jess." He followed her out of the room, took a deep breath. He wished he had a shot of bourbon; he could use the courage to say the next words. "I'm sorry."

"Yeah, that's how this started, if you remember correctly." She dropped her bag by the sofa. He saw her gaze slow over the garment bag he had laid there.

"I shouldn't have said what I did," he continued. "I just want things to be like they were before."

She trailed her fingertips over the bag and finally looked at him.

"That's what you want."

He nodded.

"Fine." She cleared her throat. "I'm not sleeping with you in the hotel. I don't care if you have to sleep in the car in the valet garage."

"Got it."

CHAPTER 31

*J*essica

He looked incredible in the tux. That pissed her off. She needed him to look like a little boy wearing his dad's suit. Or like a grumpy jerk of a chef who traded in his flannel shirts and jeans for a tuxedo. Instead, he looked like a male model, and it hurt to look at him.

Not quite clean-shaven. That delicious five o'clock shadow. His dark hair combed back neatly. The little piece that wanted to slide over his forehead. The tiny curls at the base of his neck. Even the damned patent leather shoes were perfect.

On top of that, he was a perfectly polite, interesting date. He had ushered her out of their room and to the church with a hand on her back. Smiled at her like he was madly in love with her when she happened to meet his eyes as she walked down the aisle. She didn't believe it. Not a damned bit of it. But he was good. Definitely enough to keep Miriam Buchanan off her back.

Unfortunately, good enough that her friends seemed to think this was a real thing, too. Chelsea had given her a quick little thumbs up when she had first seen them together at the rehearsal the day before and again earlier when she saw them together before the wedding. Courtney, Sabrina, and Sadie had all eyeballed the two of them curiously and shot her wicked grins when Hayes had his back turned.

The hell of it was, she had wanted a date—well, she *needed* the date to stay under Miriam's radar—to be comfortable. To feel like she fit in. Jessica had decided she liked the idea of Hayes being with her, and then she had looked forward to it, and then *that kiss*. That kiss in the kitchen when the steam between them exploded. And then that whole night of steam and skin and kissing and now she *wasn't* comfortable with Hayes.

Not with Hayes as her date. Not with Chelsea's new family. Not with the wedding guests she didn't know.

Hayes was, indeed, a dancer, too. He spun her around the dance floor song after song. Sipped champagne with her. Fetched her more champagne without her asking him, too. They shared a piece of the raspberry vanilla bean buttercream cake. Jessica's dumb traitor heart nearly flopping out of her chest when he fed her a bite and then took a bite of his own from the same fork. She had stared at his mouth for a moment, remembering the way he kissed her.

But the damned cookie table brought back other memories.

To her surprise, Hayes held his own in conversations with Rex and his groomsmen, too. Even if he did damn near growl at Rex's friend, Brody—the one who had walked her down the aisle at the church on Fifth Avenue. He smiled a time or two, killed Miriam with kindness and manners—the likes of which Jessica had *never* seen him display.

He sighed now, his warm breath rustling her hair a bit. Her feet hurt. It was late. The heels Chelsea had approved for the bridesmaids were gorgeous but certainly not made for comfort. After the rehearsal and the dinner and all day today, she was exhausted. Peopled out.

Ready to go crawl into bed. And to think she had the brunch tomorrow morning before she could go home and escape the crowd. Away from Hayes Kelley. Until Monday night when she had to go to work. And pretend that nothing had changed between them.

Maybe if she got through a few months of pretending nothing had changed she could ask for a raise. It would be hard work, after all.

"Did I tell you that you look beautiful tonight?"

His voice was gruff in her ear. Their hands clasped, his arm around her waist, they waltzed again.

"No."

"You do."

"Thanks," she mumbled, heart not in the charade anymore. Maybe after a good sleep, she would be back on it, ready to pretend to the wedding party and Chelsea and Rex's family and friends that she was madly in love with Hayes and ready to pretend with Hayes that she felt nothing toward him but that old familiar work friendship. But for now, she was done.

Hayes drew back to look her in the eyes.

"I mean it."

She stared at him silently for a moment, but she couldn't hold the eye contact. Not when everything he had done to her that night they spent together was in her mind, her heart. Not when she wanted to cup his face right now and kiss him. She could almost taste his lips, the champagne, the cake they had shared.

"Yeah." She shrugged. "Thanks."

"You okay?"

"I think I'm done." She flicked her gaze up to meet his again. "For the night."

"Okay." He nodded. Rather than wait for her at the side of the dance floor, Hayes trailed after her as she said her goodnights. She had already bid Chelsea and Rex goodnight earlier. They would leave for the Maldives tomorrow; she and Chelsea wouldn't get to catch up for a while. At least that would give her time to craft a breakup story for her and Hayes.

The elevator ride to their room was awkward. It had been hard enough earlier, when they had come down for the walk to the church, for the wedding. Now that they were heading back to their room, the one with only one bed, Jessica's belly hurt, and her palms were sweaty.

When the doors opened, Hayes ushered her out first. They walked in silence to their room, where Hayes unlocked the door. He pushed it open for her and hesitated on the threshold.

"What?" She looked at him over her shoulder.

"Do you want me to find somewhere else to sleep?"

She rolled her eyes. "You slept in here last night."

They had shared the bed last night, after the rehearsal dinner. Both had worn pajamas, and both had clung to their sides of the bed, not even accidentally bumping feet.

Hayes flinched and dragged a hand over his face and around the back of his neck.

"I don't think I can do it tonight."

Jessica tipped her head and narrowed her eyes at him.

"What does that mean?"

Hayes groaned and then stuffed his hands in his hip pockets.

"It means all I've thought about for the past twenty-four hours is sliding that dress down your body and peeling off whatever sexy-as-fuck lingerie you have on and making love to you."

She laughed softly, but even to her it sounded more like a sob.

"You had me for a minute." She shook her head. "I'd believe you want sex."

He shifted on his feet and dropped his head back to huff at the ceiling.

"You can do so much better than me, Bradshaw."

"What if I don't want to?"

"All I'm ever gonna be is the slob in the flannel and denim—"

"Don't." She cut him off with a shake of her head. "Please? Just don't."

"Don't what?"

"Don't tell me you wanna fuck me and then make excuses to me about why we can't be more than sex. You're scared, Hayes Kelley. You're scared of me."

"Didn't I just say that?"

"Not of who I am in Holly Creek. Not because I'm high society or ever will be. You know damned well, this is not who I am." She waved her hands around to indicate the city, the hotel, the glamor they'd been living the past twenty-four hours. "You're scared of me. Because I feel something. Because I made the mistake of acknowledging something that's been between us for years."

He grunted something, paced across the room to the window and kept his back to her.

"I'm not Lisa," she whispered. "It's not fair of you to believe I would hurt you like she did."

"Lisa has nothing to do with this. With us." He growled as he turned to look at her. "I don't want this life. Wedding vows. And rings. And—"

Her eyes brimmed with tears, but she made herself stand there and look at him.

"You know the sad thing, Hayes? If you had kept your mouth shut, instead of making that grand announcement that you don't love me and issuing that order to me not to love you? We would be fine. Might have taken me a bit to get over it, but we would be fine."

"No." He shook his head. "We would be just as fucked, Bradshaw."

She tipped her head back as he stalked across the room to stand by her.

"You think I would be fine? Watching you flirt with Sean? With Jax?"

"Jesus." She rolled her eyes. "They're both involved in relationships, Hayes. Flirting is nothing."

"Watching you fall for someone else? Watching you find the man to make your dreams come true? Sweep you off your feet and out of Holly Creek?"

She blinked and let the tears fall. "You don't know me. If you think I need to be swept out of Holly Creek to make my dreams come true, you don't know me at all."

"I shouldn't have kissed you." He shrugged.

"No. Guess you shouldn't have." She shook her head. "If you can't handle where we are now, you shouldn't have put us—"

He grabbed her by the shoulders and dragged her up to press against his body. Jessica lifted her hands and dug her nails into his shoulders, annoyed that he still wore his tuxedo jacket.

"I don't wanna hurt you." He kissed the corner of her mouth, his hands rough, demanding on her hips.

"Do your best, Hayes." She shook her head. "Not sure we can make things any worse."

CHAPTER 32

*H*ayes

If one night of casual sex wrecks a friendship, why not fuck it all the way up and do it again? Had he thought maybe it wouldn't be as good with Jessica the second time? That angry sex in the Plaza Hotel would be boring and remind him that they were better off just trying to salvage a working relationship?

He snorted and rolled his eyes. Nope. He knew better. He had spent the entire time in the city undressing her with his eyes, wanting to grab her away from all the men around her, all the people looking at her, and steal her away to their room. And make love to her.

Maybe he had purposely provoked her to instigate angry sex. It started rough, hard, frenzied. But it ended so very tenderly, and they had slept entwined and woke up and made love again before showering and getting dressed for the brunch.

Hayes had had enough wedding crap to last him a lifetime, but it was clear to him now that he would never have enough of Jessica Bradshaw. The hell of that? They still weren't really speaking. They most certainly hadn't gone back to the way things had been before the first kiss. They worked in the same building but only interacted when it was necessary.

Jessica had beat him to the punch, letting friends and family know they weren't dating. That Hayes had simply done her a favor and gone with her to Chelsea's wedding as a friend.

He was looking at another Christmas alone. Well, he and his dad eating chili and watching football. Which would suffice. As he well knew. But for a short amount of time, things had seemed to look up.

Hayes hated that he had made her cry. He could deal with her rage, even when she called him a *chauvinistic jerk*. But he didn't want to hurt her. He had never wanted to hurt her.

She had hit the mark. On so many points, really. Her words rattled around his head all through their silent drive home. All afternoon at his place, alone. She was right. He was projecting his fears, his hurt, over his broken engagement on Jessica. Completely unfair of him and even worse for him to lie, to claim it was simply that he didn't and wouldn't love her.

Jessica was not Lisa. Nor any other woman. She didn't need the glitz, the city, the big wedding. They had talked about it before. She liked it right here in Holly Creek. With him. And he knew that and still chose to push her away to keep his heart hidden from her.

The Chop House closed earlier for Christmas Eve. Even the bar was closed by nine. He never voiced the thought to his patrons, but he wanted to tell them they didn't have to go home, but they couldn't stay at his place to avoid family or playing Santa or whatever it might be they needed to escape from.

He assumed Jessica was in her office since her light was on. The entire drive back to Holly Creek he had stewed over this.

He was in love with her precisely because she was Jessica Bradshaw. What he felt for her had nothing to do with Lisa. With his past.

Gambling had never been his thing. He was too tight with his money. But this time, he had to take the chance. If he let things get too bent out of shape between them, she might eventually leave the restaurant, even leave the area in search of a new job.

He took a bottle of champagne from the refrigerator at the bar, hooked two flutes in his fingers, and carried them through the kitchen to her office. The Christmas music in her office made him smile, although it made him sad. He had given her such a hard time about Christmas. For years. Not even so much because he disliked it that much, but because it was too much fun to get her riled up.

The song was something modern, about slow dancing at Christmas. Fortuitous, he decided with a nod. She didn't look away from her computer screen when he peeked his head into her office.

"It's Christmas Eve," he reminded her.

"I know." She nodded. Eyes still on the computer. "Cocktails at Mom and Dad's tonight. No desire to go."

"Why not?" His voice was gruff, maybe because he felt guilty. For the things he had said to her. For the things he had done with her for physical pleasure even after telling her he didn't love her.

Finally, she turned her attention to him.

"Nolan proposed to Amelia the other night," she said quietly. "Happy for them, but just had enough wedded bliss these days."

He watched her roll her chair back and stand. She pulled her coat off the hook on the far wall and slipped it on.

"Hayes, I can't do this anymore." She met his eyes. "I love

working here. But I can't. The—whatever—" She shook her head.

"Bradshaw." He stepped into her office, champagne and glasses in his hands. "Stay."

She eyed the champagne suspiciously, and slowly, she lifted her gaze to meet his eyes again.

"No." She laughed again. "I'm not doing that again, either."

"Look." He put the glasses on her desk and peeled the foil off the neck of the bottle. "Lisa decided Holly Creek was too slow, too pedestrian for her."

"What—"

"I know. Look at Hayes Kelley using big words," he said with a self-deprecating grin. "But. Lisa was years ago, and I realized that even though you were right—that I was pushing you away because of what happened with her—it was dumb. Because the reason I fell in love with you is because you're special. You're you. There's no other Jessica Bradshaw, no one like you."

"Hayes," she whispered.

"So, I mean, I don't want a big wedding. No ten-mile-long guest list. No monkey suit. No orchestra. No big city cathedral. It worked well for Chels and Rex, but that's not us, right? I don't want to go to the Maldives. See, I think we could go to Vermont. I don't know, maybe in leaf-peeping season."

She snorted and shook her head.

"Or, maybe we could go south. Hit a beach in Florida. And save a big chunk of honeymoon money and spend it on a house. Unless you wanna stay where you are. I saw a nice fixer-upper for sale on Evergreen the other day. And while maybe we need to wait a year or something for kids, we could get a dog. Or two. Because I know you'll want a lap dog. And I want a lab. A hunting dog."

Jessica sniffled. "You don't hunt," she reminded him.

"Still. Manly dog." He shrugged. "I don't need diamonds, but I'd like to at least have a simple band. You, on the other hand? That's the one thing I will do traditionally."

"Hayes." She frowned and shook her head again. He popped the cork on the champagne and splashed the bubbly liquid into both glasses. He started to hand her a flute but put it back down when he realized he forgot something. He pulled the small ring box from the front pocket of his jeans and popped it open.

"So, if you think about it," he tipped his head and looked from the ring to her as he talked, "we've been together ten years. I'd like to say I knew it all along, that I loved you from the words *you're hired*. I did. I mean, I fell a long time ago, but I don't know when, Jess. I only knew when I *knew*."

"When?"

She maintained her distance from him, from the ring. Not ready to trust him yet.

"When I heard that you got bombed at the party. The peach schnapps got me."

"Shut up." She laughed softly.

"When I knew I was gonna go with you to the wedding, because I couldn't stand the thought of you going alone. Because I knew you would be uncomfortable with it, and that's not fair to anyone. Because then you can't give anyone the best version of you. Of Jessica Bradshaw."

"You make me feel safe," she mumbled. She made a quiet sound. Hayes wasn't sure if she was laughing or crying. "Even with all of this stupid shit between us, Hayes, I feel at home with you."

"You are," he told her. "I always want you to feel at home with me. Here. In Holly Creek."

She stared at him in silence, long enough to make his gut

clench. What if she said no? Jesus, he hadn't thought this through.

"So, I'm not even suggesting we do this right away. Maybe next year. The year after. And I'm not gonna change. I'm not gonna turn into a happy little camper or Santa's number one elf. I'm a grouch. It suits me."

He blew out a deep breath as he lowered himself to his knee.

"But I will do anything and everything to make you happy, Bradshaw." He held out the box again. "I love you."

"This is a proposal." It wasn't an answer. Wasn't a question. She wasn't laughing. In fact, she was crying again.

"This was my mom's ring," he said quietly. "I went to see Dad this morning."

"We get married in a church." She met his eyes. "Small wedding, but I do want a dress. Nothing huge, no big train. And I *do* want the church."

"Okay." He nodded.

"And we can't steal Amelia and Nolan's thunder."

"No, but we can make our own." He quirked an eyebrow at her. "Jess. Wanna get married?"

"I do," she said with a small smile. "I do."

EPILOGUE

*J*essica Wilson Kelley won the Left, Right, Center jackpot. Twice. Jessica couldn't help but catch Hayes' eyes over the dining room table. When she had invited Hayes and his dad to her parents' house for Christmas dinner, Hayes had almost balked. He had come around quickly, but not without telling her that his dad would be less than enthused about the change in plans.

She had been with Hayes when he relayed her mom's invitation to him earlier this morning. And yes, when Wilson had readily agreed, when he insisted Hayes would fix a casserole to bring, when he bid Jessica to thank her mom for the invite, Jessica had simply repeated Hayes' words.

Less than enthused.

Now, here it was, Christmas evening. Dinner had gone off without a hitch. Hayes had brought his sweet potato gratin, which had been wiped out the first time the dish was passed around. Because it was last minute, Jessica had assured both Hayes and Wilson no gifts were needed, but they'd shown up bearing gifts anyway. Wilson had brought her mom a bottle of wine, and Hayes had brought a bottle of bourbon for her dad—most likely, both were from Hayes' inventory at the Chop House.

Jessica and Amelia had helped their mom clean the kitchen, carols playing in the background. The guys had gathered in the living room to check the football score. Nolan's family Christmas was the following weekend, so he was elbow to elbow with the guys, drinking the Cocoa Noel Stout with them. Jessica's dad had ventured out the week before to get a couple of growlers of the festive beer, thinking it would be good to serve for the holidays.

Neither of her parents had expected two engagements announced this year during the holiday season.

Once the kitchen was clean, the bunch of them had joined at the dining room table again to play the card game. And Wilson—the man Hayes had muttered would not play games earlier when her mom mentioned it—had, indeed, played and won two jackpots.

Nolan hopped up from the table to get more beer. Jessica watched him as he asked everyone there if they wanted another. When she had first started waitressing, she'd had to write everything down, but she had quickly become adept at memorizing orders. Nolan nodded as each of them confirmed or turned down his offer and then disappeared into the kitchen. She wondered if he would get everything right.

The ring he had given Amelia was beautiful. A platinum band and a diamond roughly the size of Rhode Island. The two of them were planning to spend the following weekend in Philadelphia with his family for their Christmas and then fly from there to Cancun. Amelia was already making wedding plans, even though they had only been engaged five days.

Jessica didn't blame her, though she was in no hurry

herself. The last thing she wanted to do was upstage her little sister's wedding. Besides, the only thing that would change between her and Hayes when they got married was her name. They had been work spouses so long, she honestly couldn't imagine either of them finding a reason to walk away now. Not after finally ironing out the issues—Hayes' worry, his stubborn clinging to the refusal to believe in her, believe in love, after his failed engagement.

A month ago, back when Hayes and Sean and Lila Addison and everyone else in Holly Creek had been so busy trying to find Jessica a date for Chelsea and Rex's wedding, she would never have dreamt things would end up this way. But now that she and Hayes had shared so much, she couldn't imagine any other ending.

Or beginning.

She rested her hand on her belly and took a sip of her water. No one had paid much attention to her drinking water. Jessica wasn't a big drinker, so it wasn't that unusual.

"I think on that note," Amelia threw a grin in Wilson's direction, "I'm done. You wiped me out, Wilson."

He laughed as Carla pushed the pile of dollar bills in the center of the tables at him.

"What time is it?" her dad asked around a yawn.

"Mm." Hayes shifted on his chair to pat his pockets.

"It's almost nine." Jessica leaned into Hayes. "Your phone's in your truck."

He laughed when she looked up at him.

"I'm beat," Amelia announced. Jessica saw the look her sister and Nolan exchanged. Rather than make her roll her eyes, that look gave her ideas, too.

"You ready?" Nolan asked her.

"I am."

Like a football team breaking the huddle, they were

moving all at once. Chairs scooting back. All of them standing, pushing their chairs in. Amelia, Jessica, and Carla all reached for glasses to carry back to the kitchen.

"Ew." Amelia frowned when Nolan chugged the beer he had just poured.

"Now I just need a little sweet treat to go with that."

Jessica ducked her head when she overheard Nolan's quiet reply to her sister. Hayes chuckled softly.

"It does pair well with cookies." He leaned close to say the words in her ear.

"I think we should walk around and look at Christmas lights," she told him. He followed her into the kitchen when she carried the glasses to the sink.

"Why?" The deadpan expression again. Funny how it had scared her as a teenager, amused her when she came back from college, and now suddenly, it simply turned her on. Maybe it was the challenge; what could Jessica do to paint a little emotion on his face?

"Because it's Christmas night," she said simply.

"We've been looking at those same Christmas lights for over a month now," he reminded her.

"And then," she turned and cozied up to him, sliding her hands over his shoulders. "We could go to my place. And turn on my tree. And—"

"No."

She drew back and quirked an eyebrow at him.

"You don't want to make love by the tree?"

"Mmm." He grunted, but his lips perked up into a slight smile. "Yes to that. No to another Christmas movie."

"I love you, Hayes." She lifted up on her tiptoes to kiss him.

"Am I gonna have to say that to you all the time now?"

She shrugged. "Only when you mean it, I guess."

"Hmm." He took her left hand from his shoulder and

looked at it. Pressed his thumb to the diamond his mom used to wear. "I love you, too."

"Wanna set a wedding date?"

"Already?"

"Amelia and Nolan set theirs."

"Next fall. Thought you didn't want to scoop them."

"What about next Christmas?" she whispered.

"Oh, God, no. Not another—"

She raised her eyebrows and tipped her head at him.

"Absolutely," he said with a real smile. "Whatever you want, Bradshaw."

THE END

THANK you for reading Christmas And Other Inconveniences. If you enjoyed Jessica & Hayes' story, please consider leaving a review on your favorite bookish site!

BETTING ON CHRISTMAS COLLECTION

Get the entire multi-author collection this holiday, for steamy romance that's Hallmark-like with heat.

Click to get the next book in the multi-author Betting on Christmas Collection.

BETTING ON CHRISTMAS BONUS SCENES

Want more of your favorite characters from the Betting on Christmas Collection?

Your authors all have created Bonus Scenes and Epilogues for you to revisit your characters and see how their stories continue.

Click the link below or scan the QR code for the page of ALL the epilogues and bonus scenes!

Click here for the bonuses or scan the QR code below:

TRACY'S WELCOME TO KISSING SPRINGS COLLECTION

Welcome to Kissing Springs & Lockland Distilling Tie In Stories By Tracy Broemmer

Leaving You (Originally published in the Backing the Bluegrass Anthology)

Seducing You (Published in the Ride a Cowboy Anthology)

Kissing You (Coming soon in the Let's Get Naughty, Volume 2 anthology)

ALSO BY TRACY BROEMMER

Women's Fiction Novels:

Luther's Cross 10th Anniversary Edition

Fairytale (Writing as Therese Kinkaide)

Just Like Them

Small Hours

Picket Fences

Two Story Home

Green-Eyed Girl

Say Everything

Come Home For Christmas

Sketching Litchfield Lake

Ever, Again

Safe as Houses

Damsel

The Valentine Suite

Every Little Thing, Lorelei Bluffs, Book 1

Two A.M., Lorelei Bluffs, Book 2

Blind, Lorelei Bluffs, Book 3

Leaving July, Lorelei Bluffs, Book 4

Hesitation Marks, Lorelei Bluffs, Book 5

Four Letter Words, Lorelei Bluffs, Book 6

Love, Nashville, The Mississippi Queen Trilogy, Book 1

Forever, Duncan, The Mississippi Queen Trilogy, Book 2

Always, Jess, The Mississippi Queen Trilogy, Book 3

Gettin' Hitched, The H Books, Book 1

Hookin' Up, The H Books, Book 2

Holdin' On, The H Books, Book 2.5

Contemporary Romance Novellas:

Indian Summer, A Novella

Dear Jaclyn Perris, A Novella

French Stuff, A Novella, Originally included in newsletter builder anthology, Just Coffee

Holdin' On, A Novella, Originally published in the anthology, Snowed Inn

End in Flames, Rescue Me Serial Anthology

Mistletoe Mishaps

Toasted: A New Year's Eve Novella

Endless Summer, Originally published in the anthology, Cool Off (Timberton Hounds)

Homeless Holiday, Included in the anthology, Let's Get Naughty (Timberton Hounds)

Deadman's Hollow

Boone's Girl, Originally published in the anthology, Aced, Back to School

Feels on Wheels, Originally published in the anthology, Fall Into

Love (Love in Motion Duet)

Rings on Wings, Originally published in the anthology, Fall Back Into Love (Love in Motion Duet)

Intoxicate Me, A Novella (515 Whiskey)

Today, Again, A Novella, Originally included in the anthology, One Sweeet Day

Trusting Cupid, A Novella, Originally included in the anthology, XOXO

Other Novellas:

The Devy Man, A Horror Novella

Women's Fiction Short Stories:

India Falls

Luther's Cross: 87,600

The Candy Cane Tree of Willow Lane

Delays, Originally published in the anthology, Snowed Inn, Vol.2

Same Time Next Year, Included in the anthology, Sweet Sprinkles

Contemporary Romance Short Stories:

Perfect Pictures, The Wine Tasting Series, Traminette

Coming Home, The Wine Tasting Series, Edelweiss

Save Me Every Dance, The Wine Tasting Series, Rosé

Marry Me, The Wine Tasting Series, Shiraz

Birthday Wishes, The Wine Tasting Series, Muscat

Dad Jeans, The Wine Tasting Series, Vignoles

Peppermint Lane, Originally published in the anthology, Sweet Treats

Priceless Memory, Timberton Hounds Sports Romance

Truly Dante, A Mississippi Queen Trilogy short, Included in the anthology, Naught & Nice

Strawberry Wine, Originally published in the anthology, Stand For Ukraine

Love Letter, Originally published in the anthology, Hope For Ukraine

Leaving You, A Lockland Distilling Short, Originally published in the anthology, Backing the Bluegrass

Sambuca Santa, Included in the NL Builder anthology, Kissing Santa Claus

ABOUT THE AUTHOR

 Tracy Broemmer is the author of several contemporary romance novels including The H Books, Wedding Day Shenanigans, and the Mississippi Queen Trilogy. Tracy also writes women's fiction and is the author of the Williams Legacy series as well as several stand-alone titles.

Tracy's books have been called gripping, emotional, and timely, and readers describe her characters as real and relatable.

Tracy lives in Midwestern Illinois with her husband of 30 years. Visit her on the web and sign up for her newsletter at www.broemmerbooks.com

www.ingramcontent.com/pod-product-compliance
Lightning Source LLC
Chambersburg PA
CBHW022144240626
47153CB00007B/2508